D0779000

'For those who wish to find in history a key to our absolutist present.' *—Il Giornale* (Italy)

'*Stella* is a book you can hardly put down. You will read it in just a few hours, whatever you might have planned... It has a style which in a certain way echoes Hemingway's war reporting—you might call it "melancholy heroism." But it reads very well, you can't say otherwise.' *—Die Welt* (Germany)

'Würger writes in a quiet, authentic style; he writes without mercy but never without empathy, never in a way that is contrived or lurid.' *—Jüdische Allgemeine* (Germany)

'*Stella* shows how war and love sometimes bring up the worst in a human being, and how much pain love can cause.' *—Metro* (Netherlands)

'Würger avoids any hint of pathos, writing instead in clearly chiseled, artfully sparse sentences... It is the escalating state of emergency that explains everything in this slimmed down, concise novel.' *—Abendzeitung München* (Germany)

Takis Würger is a reporter working for the German news magazine Der Spiegel. Named one of Medium's 'Top 30 Journalists under 30,' alongside other accolades, Würger's work as a journalist has taken him to Afghanistan, Libya, Mexico and Ukraine. His first novel, *The Club*, won the lit.Cologne debut prize in Germany.

Liesl Schillinger is a literary critic, writer and translator, and teaches journalism and criticism. She has translated novels by Alexandre Dumas fils, Nataša Dragnić, Inès Cagnati and Lorenza Pieri, and is the author of *Wordbirds: An Irreverent Lexicon for the 21st Century*. In 2017, she was named a Chevalier of the Order of Arts and Letters of France.

Stella

Also by Takis Würger

The Club

Stella

TAKIS WÜRGER

Translated from the German by
Liesl Schillinger

Grove Press UK

First published in the United States of America in 2021 by Grove Atlantic
First published in Great Britain in 2021 by Grove Press UK,
an imprint of Grove Atlantic
First published in the German language in 2019 by Carl Hanser Verlag

Copyright © Carl Hanser Verlag GmbH & Co. KG, Munich
English translation © 2021 by Liesl Schillinger

The moral right of Takis Würger to be identified as the author of this
work has been asserted by him in accordance with the Copyright,
Designs and Patents Act of 1988.

All rights reserved. No part of this publication may be reproduced,
stored in a retrieval system, or transmitted in any form or by any
means, electronic, mechanical, photocopying, recording, or otherwise,
without the prior permission of both the copyright owner and the above
publisher of the book.

For lyric permission details, see Acknowledgments.

Parts of this story are true. The text in italics contains excerpts from
testimony used in a court trial held in Berlin. The original documents
are located in the Berlin State Archive.

1 3 5 7 9 8 6 4 2

A CIP record for this book is available from the British Library.

Trade paperback ISBN 978 1 61185 449 7
E-book ISBN 978 1 61185 890 7

Printed in Great Britain

Grove Press UK
Ormond House
26–27 Boswell Street
London
WC1N 3JZ

www.groveatlantic.com

For my great-grandfather Willi Waga,
who was gassed in 1941 as part of the
involuntary euthanasia program Aktion T4

Stella

In 1922, a judge sentenced Adolf Hitler to three months in prison for disturbing the peace, an English archaeologist discovered Tutankhamen's tomb, James Joyce published the novel *Ulysses*, Russia's Communist Party elected Joseph Stalin general secretary, and I was born.

I grew up in a villa on the outskirts of Choulex, near Geneva, with cedars in front. We had thirty acres of land and linen curtains in the windows. In the cellar there was a strip where I learned to fence. In the attic, I learned to identify cadmium red and Naples yellow by their scent and to know what it felt like to be hit with a woven rattan rug beater.

In my part of the world, you answered the question of who you were by giving your parents' names. I could say that Father was the third generation to run a factory that imported velvet from Italy. I could say that Mother was the daughter of a major German landowner who lost his fortune because he drank too much Armagnac. All schnappsed up, Mother would say, which didn't lessen her pride. She liked to talk about how the entire leadership of the Black Reichswehr came to his funeral.

At night, Mother sang lullabies about shooting stars, and when Father was traveling and Mother was drinking to ward off loneliness, she would push the dining room table against the wall, put on a record, and dance Viennese waltzes with me; I had to stretch my arm high to put my hand on her shoulder. She said I would learn how to lead well one day. I knew she was lying.

She said I was the handsomest boy in Germany, though we didn't live in Germany. Sometimes she let me comb her hair with a buffalo horn comb Father had given her; she said her hair should be like silk. She made me promise that when I was a grown man with a wife, I would comb my wife's hair. I observed Mother in the mirror, how she sat before me with her eyes closed, how her hair shimmered. I promised.

When she came to my room to bid me good night, she laid both her hands on my cheeks. When we went for walks, she held my hand. When we went hiking up in the mountains and she drank seven or eight shots up at the peak, I was happy that I could support her on the way back down.

Mother was an artist—she painted. Two of her paintings hung in our hall, oil on canvas. A large still life of tulips and grapes. And a small painting, a rear view of a girl who held her arms crossed at the base of her spine. I looked at that painting a long time. Once I tried to cross my fingers like the girl in the picture. I couldn't make it work. My mother had painted the wrists in an unnatural position that would have broken the bones of any real person.

Mother often spoke about what a great painter I would become and seldom about her own art. Late in the evening, she would talk about how easy painting had been for her in her youth. When she was a girl, she had applied to the painting school of the art academy in Vienna and failed the charcoal drawing test. Maybe another reason she was rejected was that, back then, hardly any women were permitted to study at academies. I knew I wasn't allowed to ask about that.

When I was born, Mother decided that I would attend the art academy in Vienna in her place, or at least the Academy of Fine Arts in Munich.

Definitely, I was to avoid having anything to do with the Feige-Strassburger art school in Berlin or the Röver school in Hamburg, which were thick with Jews, she said.

Mother showed me how to hold a paintbrush and how to mix oil paints. I took pains to do it right because I wanted to make her happy, and I studied further when I was alone. We drove to Paris, looked at Cézanne's pictures in the Musée de l'Orangerie, and Mother said that when anyone painted an apple, it should look like one of Cézanne's. I was allowed to prime Mother's canvases, went hand in hand with her through museums, and tried to take note of everything when she praised the depth of color in one painting and criticized the perspective of another. I never saw her paint.

In the year 1929, the stock market in New York collapsed, the Nazi Party won five of ninety-six seats in the state elections in

Saxony, and, shortly before Christmas, a horse-drawn sleigh drove into my hometown.

It slid on runners across the snow. A stranger sat in the driver's seat in a floor-length dark green loden coat. Father would never be able to find him later, despite all the assistance the police offered. It remained unclear why the man was transporting an anvil horn with him up on the driver's seat.

About a dozen of us boys were in the church square, throwing snowballs at the metal weather vane on top of the tower. I don't know who was the first to throw one at the coachman. The snowballs crossed in flight and splattered on the wood walls of the sleigh. One snowball hit the man on the temple; I thought it was mine. I hoped the other boys would like me for it. The man didn't flinch.

He reined in his pony. He took his time about it, stepped down from his perch, whispered in the animal's ear, and went up to us. As he stood before us, snowmelt dripped into his collar.

We were young; we didn't run away. Fear was something I had yet to learn. The coachman carried something short, forged, and dark in his hand.

He spoke Urner German, I think, a dialect you rarely heard in my area.

"Who threw that?" he asked softly, looking at us. I heard the snow crunch under the soles of my shoes; it was frozen over and glittered. The air smelled of wet wool.

Father had told me that telling the truth was a sign of love. Truth was a gift. Back then I was sure that was right. I was a child. I liked gifts. What love was, I didn't know. I stepped forward.

"Me."

The point of the anvil horn entered my right cheek, cut through to the jaw, and split my face open to the corner of my mouth. I lost two back teeth and half an incisor. I have no memory of this. My memory returns at the moment when I looked into Mother's gray eyes. She was sitting beside my hospital bed and drinking tea with corn liquor in it, which she poured from a flask. Father was traveling.

"I'm so glad that nothing happened to your painting hand," Mother said. She stroked my fingers.

My cheek was held together with stitches soaked in carbolic acid. The wound was inflamed. In the coming weeks, I lived off chicken broth that our cook prepared each day. At first, the broth oozed through the sutures.

The medicine made me groggy. The first time I looked into a mirror, I realized that, because of the coachman's blow, I had lost the ability to see colors.

Many people can't tell the difference between red and green, but I had lost all the colors. Crimson, emerald, violet, purple, azure, blond . . . all of them were nothing for me but names for different shades of gray. The doctors would speak of cerebral achromatopsia, of a color sense disruption that sometimes occurs to old people after a stroke.

You'll grow out of it, they said.

Mother put a sketchpad on my lap and brought me a box of paints. She had gotten them from Zurich so we could begin instruction in the hospital.

"The colors are gone," I said. I knew how important painting was to her.

Mother crooked her head, as if she hadn't heard me.

"Mama, forgive me."

She called for a doctor. I had to look at a couple of pictures and have liquid poured into my eyes.

The doctor explained to Mother that this happens sometimes, it wasn't such a terrible thing; after all, when you went to the cinema the films were always in black and white.

"Forgive me, Mama," I said, "please forgive me. Mama?"

The doctor said it was a miracle that my facial nerves had remained intact. If they had been damaged, my speech would have been impaired, and saliva would have dripped from my mouth. The doctor said something about what a lucky boy I was. Mother just sat there, taking big swigs of her drink.

Mother sent a telegram to Father in Genoa. He drove all night.

"It's my fault," I said.

"There's no blame here," he said.

He stayed in the hospital and slept on a metal cot beside me.

Mother said, "What will people think?"

Father said, "Why should we worry about that?"

When the wound throbbed, he told me stories he had heard on his journeys to the silk dealers of Peshawar. Father gave me an old metal box from Haifa, etched with a rose pattern, which he said would make your wishes come true if you stroked the top of the casing three times counterclockwise. The lid stuck. Mother said if the box didn't disappear, she was leaving.

Mother hardly touched me at all. When I reached for her hand while we walked, she flinched. When she wished me good night, she stood in the doorway and looked out the window, though it was dark outside. Soon Father left again for his travels.

After I was hurt, Mother would drink so much that she would lie down on the dining room floor, and the cook and I would have to carry her to her bedroom.

Some nights Mother climbed alone into the Alpine meadows. Sometimes she would spend two days in a row shut up with her canvases. I was eight years old and didn't know if it was because of me.

My favorite place was the lake behind the Minorite monastery. On one side it was bordered by a mossy wall, on the other by a rock face.

At the lake I'd lie down among the reeds and smoke tobacco cigarettes, which I'd made from my father's cigars.

The cook showed me how to catch trout with the help of a stick, string, and bent nail. Later the cook would gut the fish and stuff it with chopped garlic and parsley, and then we would grill it over a fire on the riverbank and eat it while it was piping hot.

The cook showed me how to suck nectar from lilac blossoms.

I helped her braid the challah and carried milk cans from the dairy to our house. Sometimes we skimmed off the cream and shared it.

At a time when other boys were making friends and bringing them home, I couldn't, because Mother was there. Perhaps I got used to loneliness because I could not miss what I did not know.

Mother drank arak, which clouded when she infused it with ice water. I would pretend she was drinking milk. There was a jetty on the lake that creaked in the summer heat. Once I stood there in the fall, on the far edge, at dawn, and skimmed flat stones across the water. When the cook and Father had no time for me, and Mother drank away her days, I felt invisible.

I looked at the rock wall that edged the lake and asked myself why I had never seen anyone jump from it.

I grabbed the tall grass and the rock outcroppings and clambered up. From the top I could look at the lake bed and see how the algae swayed. I ran to the end of the rock and farther, into the air. The impact was hard on the leather soles of my shoes, and the cold water roared in my ears. When I came to the surface, it was hard to breathe, but I had enough air left to let out a cry. I saw the waves that my impact on the water had left behind.

With dripping pant legs, I stepped onto the kitchen tiles. The cook was kneading dough and asked whose idea it had been. I didn't know what to say. Falling is something you can only do alone, I thought. I leaned against the warm oven. The cook rapped her hand, dusty with flour, on the tiles. She gave me a washcloth.

Father had them call for me that night. When he was home, he mostly sat in his library. He liked to read for hours on end: Russian novels, Eastern philosophy, haikus. I knew that Father and Mother did not love each other.

Between my fingers I twirled a flowering reed I had plucked from the riverbank.

"The priests say you jumped," said Father.

I nodded.

"Why?" he asked.

I kept silent.

"Do you know that silence is sometimes worse than lies?" he asked.

He sat me on the armrest of his reading chair.

We listened to the ticking of the clock.

"It felt good, Papa. Why does it feel so good to fall, Papa?"

He thought about it for a long time. Softly he began to hum a melody. After a couple minutes he came to a conclusion. "Because we are stupid creatures," he said.

We both were silent together. He shook his head. His hands were heavy on my shoulders, and he smelled of his books.

"What's wrong, boy? I recognize that look."

"Is Mother all right?"

He took a deep breath. "She . . ." he said. He grimaced. "Your mother . . . everything is fine, be kind to her."

I understood what he meant and that it would be easier to keep silent. Keeping silent was my way of crying.

"We can handle it," Father said, laying a hand on my neck.

I nodded. He looked at me. I knew I would jump again if I had the chance.

When I think of home, I remember the sunflowers that grew behind the house all the way to the woods beyond the hill.

Our cook didn't like sunflowers, because they had no scent, she said. The sunflower tempts bees with its beauty, she said, but has no drops of nectar at its heart, only nasty seeds.

I walked into the fields to find the scent of the flowers, and among the flower heads I felt sure that the cook was wrong. On hot summer days, when the heat burned into the pollen, the sunflowers gave out a fragrance; it was subtle, but I could smell them. And once I had recognized their scent, I smelled it again when I left the window open when I went to sleep.

It was important to have a good sense of smell. I could smell the alcohol in the hall when I came home.

I asked the beekeeper and the gardeners what sunflowers smelled like, but nobody knew. I thought it meant something, that I could smell them.

In the year 1935, Mother drank a bottle of potato schnapps when the Nuremberg Laws were announced. Mother topped up her glass a lot. I sat beside her and counted. She raised the glass to Adolf Hitler's health, calling him "Adolphe," as if he were a Frenchman.

That night, as Mother slept on the parquet floor of the ballroom, I went into the kitchen. The cook sat crying by the stove, eating freshly whipped buttercream from a wooden spoon to soothe herself. I stroked her cheek, like Father had done to me when I was little.

A few days later I overheard an argument between Mother and Father, in which she demanded that he fire the cook, whose challah she ate happily every morning. Mother called her a Jewish sow. Father said he wasn't going to fire anybody.

Mother spent more and more time with her canvases. When she wasn't painting, the canvases leaned against the wall of the attic, turned backward. Nobody was allowed to look at them.

The night after they argued, Father came to my bedside. I pretended I was asleep. He sat down cross-legged at the

11

foot of the bed and said, "My boy, one thing . . ." then there was a long pause. I wasn't sure he would finish the sentence. "The Lord created everything imaginable, do you know that? Blackbirds and elephants . . . According to Luke, God is in every creature. Do you understand, son? We must take good care of them, these creatures."

The earnestness in his voice made me uncomfortable. I didn't answer. He pinched my foot and said, "I know you're awake."

In the year 1938, the traveling exhibition "Degenerate Art" opened in Berlin, 1,406 synagogues and places of worship burned down in Germany in a single night, and in late summer I went into the sunflower field with the cook's son. We were already tall enough to see over the flowers. The cook's son was mentally disabled; he couldn't count, he couldn't remember anything, and he constantly chewed on his lower lip.

"Can you smell them?" I asked, reaching up to rest my hand on a crown of petals. The cook's son shook his head.

There was a thunderstorm that day; a lightning bolt struck an old ash tree in our garden and the rain knocked down the flowers. The gardener was gathering up flower heads to save the sunflower seeds, cursing and calling God a rotten toad.

We went through the field, the first warm drops falling on my forehead. Shortly before our house we came to the fork in the beaten path. One way led home, the other to the dairy.

As I recall, a billy goat was grazing in the dairy yard—the farmwife had tied him to a gate there. In the valley everyone knew that the goat was called Hieronymus.

His coat was white and long; he belonged to the Gletschergeiss breed. The sunshine up at the mountain peaks had blinded him years ago. I would have liked to pet him, but he bit. In the mornings, when I went to get milk, I sometimes threw him leaves from our blackberry bushes.

For the children of the valley, it was a test of courage to tug Hieronymus's horns. Once I saw the dairyman's son kick him in his soft belly.

That day, while we were running in the sunflower field, rain pattered on our faces. We made funnels out of maple leaves and drank the rainwater. I was happy about our house, that it was warm inside, and about Father, who was home in those days. I thought about what he'd said about the presence of God in all creatures and looked through the rain across the meadow up to the dairy yard. The billy goat had been standing at the gate since the morning. The first lightning bolts flashed. The cook's son cried. I took his hand and brought him to the servants' entrance of our house. Without explanation, I turned around and ran into the rain.

"Thunder," called the cook's son. "Thunder."

The climb felt easy to me, though I slipped a couple times.

I had learned to mistrust my eyes, so I wasn't surprised when the lightning bolts in the dairy yard traveled from the grass up to the sky. Thunder crashed. At the gate, Hieronymus was chewing the dirt. He had laid his muzzle on the grass and closed his eyes, as if he were waiting for death. Or maybe he was just sleeping, because the thunderstorm didn't interest him.

I untied the rope that was knotted firmly to the gate. Hieronymus lunged in my direction. I stood still. Sometimes it hurts when you do the right thing. Hieronymus bit my left hand. His teeth had fallen out years ago. He chomped into the air, then bit my right hand, which I stretched out to him. "Hey, I'm the one who gives you blackberry leaves."

Raindrops beaded his coat, which was pale and bristly. I took the rope. I laid my hand on Hieronymus's muzzle. He didn't try to bite me again; he stood still. Maybe he'd forgotten how to walk because he had been tied up too long, I thought. I knelt down in front of him in the meadow and draped him over my shoulders. His ribs pressed against my collarbone.

The billy goat was scrawny, but heavier than I'd thought he would be. He reeked of the barn. My thighs trembled.

"I'm sorry I didn't protect you when you got kicked." That day I told the billy goat things I never told anybody. How I missed my mother, even though she was there. How unconfident I felt. That I never wanted to lie, because then life would lose its meaning. On the walk down, I stumbled and scraped my knees.

As I walked down the cedar-lined path in front of our house, my pants were torn and mud was stuck under my fingernails. The billy goat had bitten my shirt collar.

Father ran to meet me on the path.

"Son."

As he hugged me, Hieronymus snapped at him.

"Didn't you see the lightning?"

I knelt on the gravel and let the billy goat slide off my shoulders. Father brushed the water off my hair. Tears came to my eyes. I was happy that he couldn't see them in the rain.

"A lightning bolt can vaporize you," said Father. Of course he could see that I was crying; he was my father.

"We must take care of all creatures," I said.

I wanted to explain to him how beautifully the lightning had flashed in the sky, and why I was happy that the coachman had come, and why sometimes I loved Mother more than him. I kept silent. And then I blurted out, so suddenly that I was startled by the sound of my voice, "You broke your word, Papa."

"What do you mean, son?"

"You said we must speak the truth. But you lie about Mother."

I saw the pain in his face. I hadn't meant to hurt him. The rainwater tasted sweet. He took my hand and went with me to the house.

As we stood in the hall, he asked softly, "Have you ever seen a hibiscus flower in bloom?" He crouched down in front of me so that he was smaller than I was. "That's what the truth is like, boy. Someday you will see it. In Egypt you will find whole gardens. It's gorgeously beautiful there. Whole gardens, where the hibiscus blooms in a thousand varieties."

Hieronymus spent the night in our greenhouse, where, by morning, he had gobbled up half the year's zucchini harvest. During the night I had gone to see him. He had let me stroke the fur at his throat.

The farmer came to get him the next morning, shook my hand, excused himself over and over again, and said he would make sure that nothing like the zucchini incident would ever happen again. He hit Hieronymus between the horns many times, with the side of his hand.

That was the year when the members of the Swiss Goat Breeders Association decided which bloodlines would be continued, a process that was officially called "breed correction." The association categorized the *Capra Sempione*, to which Hieronymus belonged, as unworthy of support.

Late in the summer, Father told me that shortly after the night of the storm, the farmer led Hieronymus out to the slurry pit and, from a distance of two meters, shot the animal between the horns with a double-barreled shotgun.

That same year, Mother summoned an eye doctor from Munich. He said that my inability to see colors had to do with my head, not my eyes. Mother believed that I just needed to try harder. She went with me to the attic.

"Now everything will be all right again," she said.

Her paintings leaned against the wall. Mother put a paint box on the table and switched around the pots of paint. Then she asked me which pot held which color. When I guessed right, she nodded. When I got it wrong, she said I just needed to concentrate. For these sessions she wore her riding boots, which she called army boots.

One of the first times up in the attic, she said, "Please, red at least, I beg you."

When Mother had been drinking, she would sometimes raise her fist, but she stuck to her resolve not to touch me.

After a few hours of lessons, a braided rattan rug beater appeared among the canvases, leaning in a corner of the attic. She said that it hurt her more than it hurt me. Every now and then the blows made me fall facefirst into the pots.

Mother said, "Wash your face before you go, please. Don't let anybody see that you've been crying."

Once I just stayed that way, with my forehead resting in the paint, and noticed that the paint pots gave off different smells. The paints were made of natural pigments. Indigo blue smelled of the butterfly blossoms in our washhouse; Naples yellow of lead; cadmium red of clayey earth in summer; black of coal; white of chalk.

I liked the coal scent best. Mother didn't give me any more instruction beyond the hours in the attic. The museum visits stopped.

Now when I had to identify colors for mother, I leaned near the tray of paints. Sometimes I took the paint pot in my hand so I could smell it better. Mother hit me less often. Once I guessed three colors right in a row. Mother stroked my index finger.

Every Saturday after the Jewish Sabbath, when it got dark, the cook held a compress of Saint-John's-wort against the scar on my face, even years after the injury. She said it would help me look elegant again. Sometimes the cook hugged me before I went to bed on those nights. I waited for it.

The cook was the fattest woman I knew. Every day she baked cakes, with blueberries in summer, apples in the fall, almonds in winter. She said her cooking was too precious for the staff, and because of that, there was always too much cake lying around. So at night she sat by the oven, playing solitaire and eating.

Once, after applying my compresses, she sat down next to me on a milking stool, gave me a plate with two pieces of honey cake, which she spread with butter, and looked at me.

"People in the house say that you always tell the truth," said the cook.

I kept silent.

"Is that true?"

"Nearly always," I said.

"Then please tell me the truth about myself."

The cook laid her hand on my head.

"Tell me, am I fat?"

Out of nervousness, I forked up a big piece of cake and shoved it in my mouth. I choked, and when the cook gave me a glass of milk, I coughed, and milk ran out my nose.

"I know that I'm a little plump, but I mean, am I fat?"

I nodded as unobtrusively as I could. It hurt her, I could see, and I didn't want that.

"Do you think that's why I can't find a new husband?" she asked.

I looked at the floor. I was sixteen years old and understood very little about men and women and why they liked each other. I shrugged my shoulders. The cook gripped me with her soft hand.

"Please tell the truth, Friedrich."

"Yes," I said.

"Do you think I'm alone because I like to eat too much?"

"You aren't alone."

"But I am fat?"

"Yes."

She exhaled. "Thank you."

"But I hurt you."

The oven was warm; we could hear wood crackling in the embers.

"Silence is worse."

We sat awhile longer on the milking stools and looked into the flames of the oven, in which a bundt cake was baking for the next day, slowly browning, until the crust began to steam. I brought down the wooden oven peel from the wall, took the cake out and put it on the kitchen countertop.

"Thank you, my golden boy, it was about to go all wrong," said the cook.

She hugged me. I pretended I didn't see her tears.

Early in 1941, as German tanks rolled through Libya as part of Operation Sunflower, Mother put up a flag with a swastika on it on the tower of our house. It was the first time in my life that I heard Father raise his voice. Father calmly told one of the stable boys to please remove the flag from the pole, then he went into the greenhouse, shut the frosted-glass door, and let out the shout that announced the end of his marriage.

From the beginning of the war, Mother wore her riding boots more and more often and drank until she lost the power of speech. One morning she lay on the floor inside the door of the house and didn't move. I called out to her, trying to wake her. She opened her eyes and looked at me; I wasn't sure she recognized me.

"Do you still love me?" she asked.

Then she wrapped both arms around my head and held me so tightly to her throat that it was hard for me to breathe.

"I am so . . ." she said. "For everything here, for everything, I am so . . ."

It was so beautiful that I got lost on my way to school.

Sometimes I wished that during the day I could forget that Mother was at home sitting on the terrace and drinking arak.

But I knew that would mean that nobody was paying attention to her and that this was my responsibility. Secretly, I sometimes laid my head against her chest when she was lying on the floor, immobile. I was checking to see if she was still breathing.

Because of the new trade embargo, Father had problems with his velvet exports. He said he would go to Istanbul and ride out the war there, but he would keep the villa in Choulex. Mother wanted to move to Munich and live off Father's money. I wanted to travel and see a little of the world. Father suggested Tehran, because there the war was far away.

During the summer I had heard stories from the stable boys about secret nightclubs in Berlin, about hustlers, cocaine, an ivory fountain in a grand hotel, and a singing Negress who rode in a coach drawn by an ostrich.

One of the stable boys had worked for a while as a horse dung collector in Berlin and said he had moved away because he couldn't stand the Berlin dialect, the "Ah" instead of "I," the "wut?" instead of "what?" It was obnoxious, he said. Even the hairdressers felt free to tell you what was on their mind.

"Is that true?" I asked.

"Everything's idiotic there, the girls, too. No culture," he said. That night was the first time I heard the rumor. In Berlin, the stable boy said, a moving truck drives into the Scheunenviertel at night and takes away the Jews. "They never come back," he said.

"Is that true?" I asked.

"It's just a rumor."

"Where is the Scheunenviertel?"

Germany seemed like a land of conquerors. The Wehrmacht controlled Europe and loomed over Moscow. The British had stopped the air raids on Berlin. Berlin, in spite of everything, was really something. A place where even the hairdressers told you what was on their minds.

I asked Father about his trips to Berlin and he gave me Theodor Fontane to read. I read the novels that were in our library and Fontane's correspondence, too. In a letter he wrote to the writer Paul Heyse in 1862, I read:

> No matter how much we like to mock Berlin, and however gladly I concede that it occasionally deserves this mockery, it cannot be denied that what happens and doesn't happen here is directly caught up in the great gear of world events. It has become a necessity to me to hear the whirring of that flywheel close by, even at the risk that it might turn into the proverbial grindstone.

At night I lay awake and thought about the word "flywheel" and about the rumor from the Scheunenviertel. In my head, the Germans were what I wanted to be. I had seen pictures of marching soldiers at the movie theater. I did not want to be a soldier, but maybe a little bit of their strength could pass to me. I asked Father about the furniture truck.

"It's something I heard," I said.

"Why are people spreading rumors?" Father's voice sounded uneasy as he answered. "I don't know, maybe it's a gray area. There must also be good Germans. I think that the truth is never more in danger than in wartime."

He turned and looked at me.

"I know what you're thinking."

I looked him directly in the face. He was trying to smile, as if it were nothing serious. I could tell he was afraid.

"Don't do it," Father said. "I beg you, not this time."

A couple of days later, Father and Mother sat together in the library, although they had long since stopped listening to each other.

"I will begin my travels with a short trip to Berlin," I said.

Mother laughed. "And what do you want to do there?"

"To see it."

"See what?"

"And take some drawing lessons."

Mother fell silent.

"You want to take drawing lessons during a war?" Father asked.

"Only for a few days."

"It's too dangerous."

"Berlin is safe."

"But there's a war."

"In the east. Not in Berlin. No bombs have fallen there for weeks."

"It's still too dangerous."

"I'm going there, Father, I want to see it. This gray area."

Father nodded and stroked his chin.

Somebody had to be able to distinguish between rumors and reality. Back then I thought I was brave.

"But it's a city of Jews," Mother said.

After Christmas, a dark-colored car with German license plates pulled to a stop on the gravel of our drive. A man in uniform stepped out. I hid in the hayloft and watched while he put his hand on Mother's backside. Later the cook would tell me that Mother had introduced the man as her nephew.

She wanted her piano and clothes to be sent on after.

The cook told me she was supposed to inform me that I should continue the exercises with the paint box. It had broken Mother's heart that I had not come to see her off.

Two years later, Mother would burn up in a garden shed during an air raid in Nymphenburg. Her nephew would say that Mother had probably drunk so much that she had mistaken the shed for the air-raid shelter.

I booked my train ticket from Geneva. The cook gave me a cap she had knitted and a woven basket that she filled with honey cakes. She hugged me. I secretly tucked my best fish-hooks into a pocket of her apron.

Father gave me a parting kiss on my forehead. "Be well," he said.

He looked like he wanted to say something else, but he kept silent.

Before he drove me to the train station, I went up into the attic and walked up to a canvas that was turned backward, leaning against the wall. For a long time I had wondered what it was that Mother painted. I turned the canvas to face the light. I went to the next one. Without haste, I turned every canvas in the attic. The canvases were bare.

The dried-up paint box was lying on the table. I took it with me. I went alone to the lake, took a rock from the shore, let it break the surface of the ice, which was still thin, and threw the paint box into the water.

January 1942

During this month, construction on the Reich Autobahn stops. In a New Year's address to the German nation, Adolf Hitler, the Reich Chancellor, proclaims his readiness for peace and calls U.S. President Franklin Delano Roosevelt a warmonger. All the skiing events at the world championships in Garmisch-Partenkirchen are canceled, to put the skiers at the disposal of the Wehrmacht. The temperature in Munich drops to −22.9 degrees Fahrenheit. The first of Dr. Joseph Goebbels's Ten Commandments for Every National Socialist is issued: "Germany is your Fatherland. Love it more than anything else, and more in deeds than in words." In Berlin restaurants, a military menu is introduced, which includes beans and horsemeat and is intended to resemble the fare of soldiers on the front. Benno von Arent becomes Reich Commissioner for Fashion; shortages of cloth present a challenge to this office. The Reich's Whole-Grain Bread Committee circulates a magazine ad with the text: "Whole-grain bread is better and healthier." In Louisville, Kentucky, USA, a young housemaid gives birth to a baby boy and names him Cassius Marcellus Clay Jr. In Wannsee, 4,529 linear miles to the east, SS Obergruppenführer Reinhard Heydrich convenes a conference. There, the skilled mechanic Adolf Eichmann lists methods for the extermination of the Jews of Europe. Once the plan is agreed, the men drink cognac and look out on the lake.

*

I reached Berlin early in the morning on the day after New Year's. The eggs at breakfast in the dining car were overcooked and tasted of fish. I went from the Anhalter Station to the Brandenburg Gate. The streets were wide and you couldn't see where they led. Berlin smelled of coal, hard soap, and boiled turnips. When I went into a restaurant and ordered a glass of Chasselas, the waitress said, "Wut?"

The ivory fountain in the hotel lobby was smaller than I had hoped. The bellboy greeted me with the word "Excellency." I was relieved that he didn't give a Hitler salute. In the lobby a newspaper salesman and a florist stood behind their stands. The head porter wore a frock coat, had combed-back wavy hair and vertical worry lines on his cheeks, and greeted me by name with a hearty handshake. The bellboys wore tailcoats and glossy ties. The elevator operator had only one arm. I gave him my basket of honey cakes. As the man turned to shake my hand, I saw that he wore a cloth armband with a swastika on his remaining arm.

I moved into my room and set up my easel, which I had sent ahead, along with a travel wardrobe trunk, by the south window. I had carried my charcoal pencils with me in my traveling case, in an old cigar box of my father's lined with cotton.

That afternoon I went to the Scheunenviertel. I saw Orthodox Jews with their black hats and black coats and stood in the shadow of the gaslights until nightfall. The next day I drank chicory coffee in a restaurant in the Hackescher Market and looked out the windows at the cars driving by. The next day I sat on the steps in front of the Berlin Stock Exchange until my toes got cold. I didn't see a moving truck.

On the first Monday of the year, carrying a leather backpack, I went to the Feige-Strassburger art school in Nürnberger Street behind the Kaufhaus Des Westens department store. The facade was ornamented with stucco, which had crumbled in spots because of the dampness of the masonry.

Before I entered, I stood for a moment on the opposite side of the street and thought about Mother. I thought of Father and of the parting words he had not spoken.

The doorknob was made of brass.

The woman at reception wore glasses with smeared lenses. I said I would like to study drawing.

"Would you like to join a drawing session right now?"

"It's that easy?"

"Today is an open workshop, a nude study. You really can't go wrong. You simply have to decide for yourself how you want to see."

Five men were sitting at easels, drawing, in a room that smelled of oil paints. I paused a moment at the door and looked across the room.

In the corner stood a tiled stove, which was cold because of the coal shortage. My breath formed clouds. On the rough floorboards I saw gray flecks of paint from the attempts of other men to capture reality in this room. The floorboards creaked, but nobody looked at me. I kept my coat on as I sat down at an empty easel.

My fingertips were numb; I breathed on them. My face was hot in spite of the cold. Everyone was looking at the front of the room.

The fur she was lying on was dark, too luxurious for a room in this art school and for the times we were living in.

The woman lay on her side, supporting her chin on one hand, and looked beyond everyone into the emptiness of the room. From time to time she coughed.

I looked at her. How her hair fell. The line that emerged between her shoulder and her wide hip bones against the darkly painted wall, the way her skin caught the light.

She was a little fuller than the ideal standard of beauty, particularly in the knees.

I thought of the painting of a naked woman by Peter Paul Rubens I had seen at the Louvre with Mother when I was a boy. I'd forgotten the title.

Sometimes the woman on the fur smiled fleetingly; I noticed the gap between her front teeth. But her face wouldn't have looked right smiling in a picture. This face would be most beautiful when the woman cried.

Near me, at the other easels, students sat and drew. The charcoal rubbed off on my fingers. Briefly I screwed up an eye and tried to see the woman as form and surface. I liked her little nose. I tried to remember how drawing worked.

After a few moments, I simply stared at her. I hid my scar behind the easel.

At the end of the hour she got up and took a cotton sheet that a man held out to her. She didn't wrap herself up in it; she just folded it and draped it over one arm. She walked out of the room naked.

I rolled up the empty sheet of drawing paper and put it in my backpack.

Later the woman stood outside, dressed now, and surrounded by three men, who were making jokes and being loud about it. She was smoking and looking across to the other side of the street. I nodded goodbye. She didn't see me.

The wind blew through my coat but hardly bothered me as I walked to the tram stop. It started snowing again, delicate flakes.

Along the way, I saw a poster on a building of a light-haired woman who bore a resemblance, I thought, to the girl in the art school. On the poster it said: "The German woman does not smoke, the German woman does not drink, and the German woman does not wear makeup!"

*

Cases #2 to #13:   *Frau S. with 4 children*
                                 Frau K. with 2 children
                                 Frau G. with 1 child
                                 Frau H. with 1 child
                                 Witnesses: 1. Gerda K., 2. Elly L.

Witnesses Gerda K. and Elly L. were employed with the accused by the Siemens company, though they were illegal residents. By day they resided with Aron P. at 152 Schönhauser Allee. They went to 24-35 Lothringer Street to visit a certain Frau S. They found the apartment under seal. From the resident Willi I., diagonally across the way, they learned that the accused and Rolf I. had observed the S. apartment—where numerous illegal Jewish residents associated—for an extended period of time. One day, in the presence of the accused and Rolf I., the Gestapo collected the following Jews from the apartment:

> *Frau S. with 4 children*
> *Frau K. with 2 children*
> *Frau G. with 1 child*
> *Frau H. with 1 child*

These persons were deported to Auschwitz. When the witness K. arrived at Auschwitz herself shortly thereafter and inquired after them there, she learned that all of them already had been gassed.

Pp. II / 162–163
Pp. I / 16, 38, 182, 184

*

The tram rumbled and squealed; the windows inside were fogged over. I sat on a seat by a window, wiped off a space with the flat of my hand, and rested my forehead on the cold glass. Outside I saw men in uniform and jackboots, women in coats that reached to the ground, publicity pillars covered with posters advertising Persil ("Wash Your Laundry in Well-Being"), cameras ("Unfettered Photography with Zeiss Ikon Kleincameras"), and something I didn't recognize that was supposed to increase feminine breast size ("A Beautiful Bust with Rondoform").

Flags with swastikas flew from every pillar and on many buildings. A double-decker bus that said "Coca-Cola" on it drove past. Steam came from the manhole covers. A woman with a star on her coat stood near me on the tram. She stood, though there were hardly any passengers on the tram and many seats were free.

"Please sit down," I said.

She shook her head.

"I beg you."

"I'm not allowed."

I felt ashamed because I was permitted to sit and averted my eyes.

I wondered how to shake off the feeling of loneliness that had come over me ever since I'd stepped off the night train. The flags, the high buildings, the people wearing stars, the noise, the smell—everything was strange to me. From a distance the Germans had seemed big; up close they were as small as I was. Only the backdrop was big—above all, the flags. The German flags were very big. I resolved to resume my travels soon.

She sat down beside me noiselessly, so near that the fur of her coat tickled my hand.

I turned and looked into her eyes. She was young, practically still a girl.

The way she was sitting, she couldn't see my scar. Quickly I looked to the side and saw my reflection in the windowpane. I didn't dare turn toward the woman, because then she would see my face. Her shoulders had fallen forward as if she were shivering. Her breath smelled of kirsch. She stroked my sleeve.

"So beautifully soft," she said.

I didn't know what to say. For a while we sat in silence next to each other.

"May I please see how you drew me?" she asked. She spoke in Berlin slang, abbreviating words and speaking with a strong accent, which made it hard for me to understand her sometimes at first.

I did nothing, just sat there and shook my head. A package of coffee beans lay in her lap; she held it tightly with both hands.

"Look, I got a whole package of coffee beans for posing."

She plucked a piece of fluff off her fur. I thought of the empty sheet of rolled-up drawing paper that stuck out of my backpack. I hadn't been able to draw her, and now I didn't dare speak to her. She had spoken to me as if it meant nothing. I felt dizzy. Slowly I leaned forward, rested my forehead on the seat back in front of me, and felt the varnished wood.

Her hand gripped my shoulder. She touched me as if she understood everything.

When I stood up, far too long before the next stop, she got up, too. She was smaller than me; seated, we had been closer in size. "Goodbye," I said, and pushed past her. My knee brushed her thigh. She followed me through the car and held on firmly to the back of a seat. Along the way, as she passed the woman with the Jewish star, she paused, glanced at the package of coffee in her hand, looked around, and pushed the coffee to the woman's chest. She didn't say a word and kept going until she stood next to me by the door of the tram.

"Do you know that woman?" I asked.

She shook her head.

"But isn't that dangerous?"

"What?"

"Helping a Jew."

She considered for a moment. She smiled, but only briefly, then her face grew serious.

"I'm Kristin." She held out her hand to me.

"Friedrich."

For a moment we stood face-to-face and held on to each other. The tram rumbled on. My palms were damp. Kristin looked me up and down. I looked at my shoes.

I kissed her hand and said, "Excuse me for failing to introduce myself. Kindest greetings, miss."

She smiled and curtsied. "Well, whaddya know? A Swiss man. Kindest greetings."

She had noticed my accent. I felt a little proud as I bowed.

"With an honest-to-goodness Swiss passport?"

Nobody had ever asked me that. I bowed again. Kristin's face changed again; it had something to do with her eyes, maybe the width of her pupils. She came a step closer to me.

"A Swiss man in Berlin," she said, and then: "Why didn't you admit that you drew me? You were sitting in the back, on the right. As I recall."

She had noticed me.

She swayed a little as the tram came to a stop and grabbed my hand.

"It was nice to meet you," I said. "Here's where I get off."

"Do you do that a lot, not answer questions?" she asked.

She held tight to my shoulder on the steps and got off with me. Her coat was too big for her, her hands were hidden deep in the sleeves; the hem must have been taken up many times and hovered just above the snow. She pressed my arm against her chest. She said she also had dizzy spells now and then, like when I leaned my head on the seat back, and that it was because of the way the tram swayed.

She insisted on carrying my backpack and said she would escort me home. Nobody had ever said that to me before.

"But you're a lady," I said.

"What's that supposed to mean?"

"I am supposed to escort you home."

"Don't be stupid," she said.

As we walked underneath the Brandenburg Gate, driving snow blew down the streets and swastika flags snapped in the wind. Kristin walked beside me with her little steps. I watched her out of the corner of my eye.

"Your papers!"

A policeman blocked our way. There were often identity checks in front of the hotel, because Jews weren't allowed to enter the government district. The head porter had called it the "Jew ban," shrugging his shoulders.

Kristin sighed as we stopped.

The policeman glanced at my passport for two seconds. "I said your papers."

"I'm Swiss, I only have a passport."

"A foreigner in the Reich," said the policeman, and brought his face right up to mine.

"Give me your identity card, and make it snappy."

"I'm . . ."

Kristin thrust her identity card between our faces. "Start with mine, Herr Kommissar."

I could see inside her open purse; there was a book by Benjamin Constant. Later I would learn that it was forbidden. The policeman turned to her. At that moment she pushed her fur hood back and her fair hair gleamed in the light of the gas lamps.

"Well?" she said, leaning her head to the side a bit and smiling at the policeman.

The man shifted his weight from one foot to the other. He tapped his cap. "Do you think that's going to work on me, darling?" He put a hand on his nightstick. "Identity cards, I said."

Kristin clutched my fingers. Inhaling sharply through her nose, she said, "Do you know who you're dealing with?"

"Are you drunk, miss?"

I felt small next to the two of them. Kristin's voice grew louder. She said the next sentences with almost no trace of her Berlin accent: "Standing before you is SS Obersturmbannführer Franz Riedweg, staff surgeon at the SS main office."

"Staff surgeon?" asked the policeman.

"At the SS main office."

The policeman's glance traveled back and forth between Kristin and me. I tried to look at him but kept averting my gaze. I was holding my passport in my hand; my real name was on it.

"But . . ." said the policeman.

"Tell me *your* name," said Kristin.

"My name?"

"I will report you. You are a disgrace to the Fatherland. To treat an Obersturmbannführer this way. Shame on you."

"But . . ." The policeman turned to me. "But, Herr Obersturmbannführer, you aren't in uniform. How was I to . . ."

"Naturally he's not in uniform," said Kristin, "it's Monday."

Then she walked past the man, pulling me along after her. I didn't understand what she was doing. It wasn't illegal for a Swiss citizen to be in Berlin. The policeman couldn't do anything to us, apart from intimidate us. But to pass yourself off as a member of the SS without being one, that was life-threatening.

"I'll just show him my passport," I said softly to Kristin. She pulled me along with her.

"Keep going and keep quiet," she said.

"But he'll arrest us."

"Nobody is going to get arrested here."

I hoped she wouldn't notice how much my hands were sweating.

After maybe fifty steps, once we knew the policeman was going to let us go, Kristin jabbed her elbow into my ribs. She smiled at me. A snowflake landed on her nose and melted.

"Why don't they wear uniforms on Mondays?" I asked.

She grinned and shrugged her shoulders.

"So where is it that you live here?" she asked.

I pointed across Pariser Platz, to the Grand Hotel. She stopped and let go of my hand. Quickly I rubbed my palm on my pant leg to dry it.

"Not seriously." She coughed with her mouth closed, grabbed my arm and linked hers through it. "Are you on vacation?"

I nodded.

"At that hotel?"

"Yes."

"Kind of expensive, isn't it?"

I kept silent.

At the revolving door Kristin took her leave with a curtsy.

"Next time you'll show me your drawing of me, won't you? And will you come Sunday night to the Melodie Klub? I sing there."

"But I can't dance."

"You can't dance?"

"No."

"Why not?"

"I've only ever danced with my mother, when I was little."

"When you were little?"

"Yes."

"Well, you're still pretty little, it seems to me."

She turned around and was about to leave.

"I didn't draw you," I said quickly.

She laughed out loud and turned toward me again. Her expression was curious and friendly.

For a moment all was quiet.

"How do you mean?"

"I couldn't do it."

"Why not?"

"I just looked at you." My heart was pounding. "I . . ."

She laid her fingers on my cheek. I fell silent. Her hand was dry.

"All right then." She ran her thumb across my eyebrow, curtsied, and started to leave.

"Could I escort you part of the way?" I called out after her.

She turned toward me again and said, "No, Fritz."

She inserted a Juno between her lips and lit it with a match. She held the cigarette between her index finger and her thumb.

She walked along the boulevard beneath the bare trees, down the middle, amid the gravel and snow. Her steps were short, and she couldn't walk a straight line. She took a bottle from the inside pocket of her coat and drank as she walked. The tips of her feet curved slightly inward. Once I felt sure she wouldn't, she turned around and waved at me, her right arm outstretched.

I crossed to the other side of the street and walked in the direction she'd gone, wanting to see her a moment longer. She turned around one more time, looked at the empty entrance of the Grand Hotel and searched for me. She paused for a couple seconds as if to catch her breath, took a compact mirror from her coat pocket, snapped it open, looked at herself in it, and adjusted her curls. She bowed her head and stood still. She let her cigarette fall.

It was as if Kristin were falling asleep on her feet. Then she woke up. She raised her head, straightened her spine, threw her shoulders back, and held her chin high. She headed down the boulevard in a westward direction, her steps long and sure.

*

Case #16: S.
Witness: Gerhard S.

Georg S. was looking for the documentation bureau in Grunewald. The accused was standing in front of the door of the office and explained to him, "Everything is fine, you need only wait in another room for the papers, then you will be served." At the instigation of the accused, S. was apprehended along with other Jews and delivered to the Grosse Hamburger Strasse internment camp, and later was killed at Auschwitz.

Pp. I / 2
Pp. I / 158, 159
Pp. I / 158

*

For two weeks I went to the drawing school, studied in my hotel room, visited museums, tried not to think about Kristin and thought about her just the same. I spent a lot of time in the Scheunenviertel. After the two weeks were up, I bought myself a train ticket to Istanbul and decided I still wanted to say goodbye to Kristin.

I asked the one-armed elevator operator if he knew about the Melodie Klub. He asked me if I knew that such establishments were illegal.

"Negro music, sir," said the elevator operator. "Totally overrun with Jews, sir."

"Music is music," I said.

"If sir says so," said the elevator operator.

That night when I entered my hotel room, there was a card hidden under the paperweight on the secretary desk on which someone had written the name of a street, a house number, and the word "Moabit." Right next to it was written: "Be careful!"

On Saturday night I went to the address. A War Committee poster hung on an advertising pillar in front of the hotel: "Conserve soap, it is made from much-needed fat and oil that now are in short supply. Never leave soap in the wash water! Never hold soap under running water! Avoid excess foam! Keep the soap dish dry! Never throw away soap scraps! Help yourself by using brushes, sand, pumice, wood ash, cigar ash, straw (field grass), and through frequent washing in warm water!"

It was the era of exclamation points.

Berlin was loud: the midnight clanging of the Church of the Redeemer, the hoofbeats of a carriage horse. From a pub came the music of a fiddler and the stamping of the soles of dancing shoes. On the street, cars with shrieking wood-powered engines drove past.

I wandered into a quiet, sand-strewn street lined with chestnut trees and drank in the crisp night air.

Factory buildings made of vitrified bricks stood on the street. The building where the club was supposed to be was dark. When you stood right in front of it, you could hear faint noises. I pressed an ear to the door. It wasn't locked. I crossed the entrance hall and took a staircase down that ended at a steel door. A plaque was screwed into the steel that read: "Swing Dancing Forbidden—Reich Chamber of Culture." From within I could hear the sound of a saxophone. The hinges were oiled.

Inside, a kind of jazz group was playing: a pianist, a drummer, a double bassist, and a saxophonist. People were dancing to a slow song. In the half dark I saw a zinc bar. Behind it stood a woman in a white shirt and suspenders. She was delicate, with erect posture. As I came nearer, I saw that her face was sprinkled with freckles, though it was winter. The air was hot. This was the Berlin I had hoped for. The club had no windows.

Dark rooms always put me at ease.

I sat at a table in the corner. There was a greyhound on the floor.

In a little while the door opened. A man came in. He was so tall that he had to duck his head. A felt hat was sunk low on his face; his coat looked as if it had been cut for him. He was carrying something in his hand that was wrapped in paper. I saw the greyhound open an eye. As he walked in, the drummer switched to a faster rhythm, probably just a coincidence.

The man cracked a broad smile. Everyone looked at him. To the beat of the music he walked up to the bar; the woman with the freckles ran to him. He used her momentum to spin her onto the dance floor. The musicians played a whole song just for him, or so it seemed to me. He danced with his eyes closed, then he kissed the woman, dropped her hand, spun on his heel, and walked in my direction. I felt my heart pounding. As he came nearer, I saw that beneath his hat he had light hair that fell onto his forehead. He was older than me, thirty years old probably, but his smile reminded me of a schoolboy's. He had no scar on his face.

He knelt on the floor beside me and took a piece of raw, bloody beef out of its wrapper. A pistol was concealed in a holster on his belt. The greyhound gobbled up the meat. The man looked around the room, then his glance rested on me.

"May I?" he asked, and gestured to the chair next to mine. I was struck by his high, brittle voice, which didn't match the rest of his body. He sat up very straight.

"Has anyone ever told you that you have unbelievably beautiful eyelashes?" He pointed to my eyes.

I nodded by mistake—obviously nobody had ever said that to me.

"And a friend of forbidden music, too?" he asked.

I couldn't help looking at his hands. He was wiping blood off himself with a white cloth.

"I mean jazz. Do you like jazz?"

"I'm just here to meet a friend."

"Outstanding," said the man, and raised a glass. He must have brought it in half full inside his coat pocket. It was a brandy glass made of crystal. "To acquaintances." As he drank, he winked at me over the edge of his glass. There was blood stuck under the nail of his left middle finger.

We listened to the musicians for a while. A southern-looking woman with a high voice sang:

> *When dawn comes to waken me,*
> *You're never there at all.*
> *I know you've forsaken me*
> *Till the shadows fall.*

"Did you know that Porter hasn't written for years? Yes? Ever since the riding accident?" The man spoke softly, as if he were afraid of being overheard. "Do you play an instrument?"

"I used to play the viola, but not well," I said.

He looked at my fingers, then grabbed my fingertips. It had been a long time since I had held a viola in my hand.

"We absolutely must play together. Are you Swiss?"

I nodded.

"Where from?" he asked.

"From Geneva."

"Ah, Geneva. The Grand Théâtre, let's drink a toast to that."

The man ordered a bottle of cognac. He said he'd had a governess from Switzerland and for that reason liked the accent. He currently employed a housekeeper from Lausanne. Then he talked about how Cole Porter had studied law at Harvard and about whether the shape of his nose revealed something about his intelligence. The man talked a lot.

At some stage he paused and asked, "What do you do?"

"How do you mean?"

"What do you do with your life?"

"Just travel," I said. "I'm traveling."

"Outstanding," he said. "What else?"

"Nothing."

"You must be doing something."

"A little drawing. And you?"

"Not so fast. Why do you do that?"

"Why am I learning to draw?"

"Yes, old boy, why are you learning to draw, yes."

For a moment I sat there and thought. The man looked at me.

"I couldn't do it for a long time. I feel safe when I'm drawing," I said. "In the pictures, I am secure, you know?"

"No."

I'd never met a man with such a commanding presence before. The man stroked my collarbone.

"I think I like you," he said.

I knew that he was superior to me in every way.

As he left the cellar to go outside by the door to relieve himself, the freckled barmaid came to my table.

"Are you friends with von Appen?"

Von Appen. I shook my head. "No," I said.

"Is he really a Moravian prince?" she asked.

"Sorry, I don't know."

"At least a baron, I heard."

"I don't know."

"Do you know anything about him at all?"

I kept silent.

"How about the horse story?"

I shook my head.

"You must know the story about the horse."

"Sorry."

She grabbed the lapel of my jacket with one hand and came so near my face that I could feel the warmth of her breath.

"So, here's the horse story, pay attention: he once turned up among the Polacks somewhere in East Prussia as the Second Panzer Division was rolling through, shooting everyone in sight, only a couple of Poles were left. Dirty dogs, those Polacks. I heard they hid stick grenades in socks, dipped them in pine sap, and stuck them under the Panzers. The cowardly swine. So one night, von Appen shows up. And here it comes: he rides into the camp of the Second Panzer Division on a black horse, like the Grim Reaper. Some people say it was a white horse, as if that really mattered. He turns up looking like the Grim Reaper, in any case. He's not wearing a uniform and he's unarmed, except for a saber. He has only this saber, hidden in his belt. He says he's there because he wants to take on the partisans. All alone. The Grim Reaper with his horse and his saber . . . Supposedly he can see at night like an owl. And boy, can he ride. He dances Viennese waltzes like a devil and can play the violin like an angel. Anyway, so he rides up to the commandant's tent and says . . ."

Von Appen laid his hand on my shoulder. The freckled barmaid took fright.

"Wartime fairy tales?" he asked with a wink. "The word is 'commander.' A commandant travels by ship."

The girl kissed him on the cheek and went back to the bar.

"Is that true?" I asked.

"The bit about dancing like a devil, yes," said von Appen.

"And the thing about the saber?"

"Of course not."

"Why the story, then?"

"People love stories like that."

"It's a lie."

"Precisely."

We didn't immediately notice when Kristin arrived on-stage. She sang the songs in a breathy voice, occasionally off-key. She sang in English with a Berlin accent. She wore a peacock feather in her hair and a polka-dot dress that stretched across her hips. After the third song she looked at us.

"Gosh," said von Appen. "She's something else, isn't she? What a knockout."

He tapped his ankle to the beat against the leg of his chair.

"I'm Tristan."

"Friedrich."

"She's got tits that could put your eye out," he said.

"Don't talk that way about her."

"That's Muck," said Tristan, as if nothing had happened, and pointed to the greyhound. "Italian Greyhound."

I nodded. I didn't dare ask what his dog had been doing in this club without him.

Tristan bent down and ruffled his ears. "One of the best breeds of all. Has to run twenty kilometers a day. Do you like dogs?"

"No," I said.

Tristan laughed as if it were a joke.

"May I ask you something, Herr von Appen?"

"Tristan. Anything."

"What do you do?"

"Nothing at all. Just live."

Kristin came up to our table from the stage. She greeted me with a kiss on my scar. It gave me goose bumps.

She whispered in my ear: "You're here." I caught a whiff of gasoline and licorice: it was the scent of the Ballistol gun oil I knew from home, but maybe I was imagining things. She tucked a pale lock of hair behind her ear; it immediately fell forward again.

You're here.

Kristin curtsied to Tristan; it came off as if she meant it ironically. He took her hand in his slender, manicured fingers and kissed it. The blood under his nails had disappeared.

"I've been admiring you," he said.

"Thank you," she said.

"Was that 'Moonglow'?" asked Tristan.

She laid an index finger on her half-closed lips. "Forbidden," she whispered, and laughed.

"Outstanding," said Tristan.

The rest of the evening I listened. I was happy to be allowed to observe Kristin's dimples from close up, and I liked the elegant way Tristan moved his hands as he talked about swing beats. He thumped me on the shoulder again and again, as if we'd known each other for years. Kristin ordered me a ham sandwich from the bar and ate it herself. She laid her finger on my knee. Nobody had touched me that way before.

She ate chocolates that she took from her purse. She bent the brim of Tristan's hat. She drank fast and let us pay. Tristan got drunk. He had to lean against the edge of the table for support.

It was a cold morning.

When we left the club, there was a coating of frost on the windowpanes of the building. Kristin linked arms with both of us. Tristan swayed. Kristin walked straight ahead. The dog pattered along beside us. Tristan had slipped his cognac glass back into his coat pocket. He got into his car, which was parked in front of the club, lifted the dog onto his shoulder and stroked the skin behind its ears. "*Aut viam invaniam aut faciam,*" he said, and pointed to me. "Who said that?"

I said nothing. Tristan started the motor.

"Hannibal. Nighty-night," he said, and put his hand on mine and stroked it. "How are you feeling?" he asked.

He drove off without waiting for an answer. His windshield was half covered in ice.

"Sleep well, you lush," Kristin called out after him.

She pulled me along the frozen sidewalk and kissed me three chestnut trees later. I kept my eyes open. She clutched my suspenders with her hands. "*Inveniam,* not *invaniam,*" she said. "What a show-off." She stroked the hair at the nape of my neck. She smelled of smoke and alcohol, and her nose was cold. She shook from coughing. It didn't bother me, because when she coughed, she laid her head on my shoulder. She held me tight. She was good at hugging. I felt sick from cognac, but I wanted this night to keep on going. Kristin stroked my cheek.

"My Swiss man," she said.

"I used to feel invisible sometimes," I said.

"You are so peculiar."

"As if I weren't there."

I felt her hand glide under my coat, up to my neck.

"Now you're with me."

I threw my coat around her to keep her warm. Before she gave me the last kiss of the morning, I asked her something I'd been thinking about for hours.

"'Moonglow,'" I said.

"Yes."

"Why is it forbidden?"

"It's by Benny Goodman."

"And?"

Her hand on my neck held me tight.

"He's a Jew," she said.

She removed her hands from my coat, took a step back, pressed her index finger against her lips and laid it on my mouth. She went off alone into the morning.

*

Cases #18 to #21:   *Chaim H. with wife and two children*
                                      Witness: Else W.

The accused entered the Weidt Workshop for the Blind, Berlin C2, 39 Rosenthaler Street, which principally employed Jews who lived there in hiding. On the following day, at the behest of the Gestapo who had been informed by the accused, all the Jews were apprehended and delivered to the Grosse Hamburger Strasse internment camp, among them Chaim H., who was discovered

hiding with his wife and two children in a room con-
cealed by a clothes closet. The H. family was taken with
other Jews to Theresienstadt and Auschwitz and has
been missing since then.

Pp. I / 10, 217, 218

February 1942

The U.S. government radio agency Voice of America broadcasts its first program in the German language. The naval theater of war of the German fleet this month: the North Atlantic, the West Atlantic, the Mid-Atlantic, the South Pacific, the Southwest Pacific, the Central Pacific, the Norwegian Sea, the North Sea, the Mediterranean, the Baltic Sea, the Indian Ocean, the Black Sea, the Bay of Biscay. Jews in the German Reich are forbidden to own pets. Glenn Miller receives the first gold record in music history for the song "Chattanooga Choo Choo." The second commandment of Dr. Joseph Goebbels's Ten Commandments for Every National Socialist is issued: "Germany's enemies are your enemies. Hate them with your whole heart." In Los Angeles, the Oscars are awarded; Walt Disney wins in the Short Subject (Cartoon) category. In Austria, the smallholder Blasius Diegruber and his wife, Anna, from the village of Russbach, are sentenced by the Special Court of Salzburg to one to two years in prison for illegal animal slaughter. In his diary, Goebbels notes: "We must provide the chance of relaxation through pleasant radio music, literature of the light variety, and the like." Italian restaurants receive instructions to serve meat dishes only on Saturdays. From Beuthen, in Upper Silesia, the first train of Jews departs for Auschwitz.

*

I let my ticket to Istanbul expire. I devoted the next days to trying to complete the assignment a teacher in the art school had given me: draw an apple.

I placed it on the windowsill. The teacher had said that an apple should be treated like a simple object. I tried to find the core shadow of the apple, the darkest spot, to give the picture a focus. As a child I'd drawn dozens of apples—it's an exercise for beginners—but now I thought of Cézanne and the way he had painted apples. At noon on the third day, I ate the apple.

In the secretary's office at the art school, I asked after Kristin. I didn't even know her last name.

"Are you one of her Latin students?" asked the secretary, whose glasses were so smeared this day that I wondered how she could recognize me. The woman must have seen the confusion in my eyes. "Miss Kristin tutors some boys from the Latin school."

"Are you sure?"

"No, I'm not sure. Nobody is sure. But last I checked Miss Kristin was an ace at declension."

"Do you know her last name?"

She pondered for a moment. "No idea. Sorry, I've never even given it a thought."

I went back to the Melodie Klub next and asked the barmaid.

"Nobody named Kristin sings here," she said.

When the telephone rang in my room and the head porter said that a Herr von Appen was standing in the lobby, I felt my pulse pound in my temples. It was two weeks after the night at the Melodie Klub.

Tristan was leaning against a marble pillar in the lobby, reading the *Schwarze Korps* newspaper.

"How are you feeling?" he asked. His handshake was soft. I had felt so lonely over the past days that I almost could have hugged him. He'd combed a part into his hair and was wearing a double-breasted suit of pin-striped wool. The waitresses who hurried across the carpet of the lobby stole stealthy glances at Tristan and smiled when he noticed them. He smelled like crisply ironed starch and a little like the Naples yellow in my paint box. I didn't ask how he'd found me.

"How was your night? Things been hopping?"

I looked at the carpet.

"A round of Pervitin can knock out an elephant," he said.

"What?"

"Those chocolates little Kristin eats all the time, they're packed with Pervitin."

Tristan laid an arm on my shoulder. It felt warm. I thought, that's how Germans are.

He walked with me through the lobby and left me only when we stood in front of a dark-colored Volkswagen. Tristan got in and opened the passenger-side door from inside. I didn't know where we were driving but I liked being with him. He was easy to be with. He moved the whole time, a little bit as if he were listening to music.

"Rosewood," said Tristan, and tapped the dashboard.

He steered carefully through the empty streets of Berlin to Savignyplatz, humming all the way.

When he got out, he stood near the wall of a house, looking at a motionless squirrel that was crouched on the ground in front of him. Tristan sank down on his haunches and lifted it up.

"What's wrong, sweetheart?" he said.

Squirrels are shy animals, but this one seemed to have no fear of Tristan.

"Show me how a man treats animals, and I'll tell you if his heart is in the right place," he said.

In the hall of the house, a porter greeted us with a bob of his head. Near the front door hung an enameled sign that said: "Entrance for Nobility Only!"

Tristan's apartment was too big for one man living alone. It was light and stuccoed; the dining room table was long enough for a dinner party. A violin stood on the tabletop, leaning against an empty flower vase. Chandeliers hung in the corridor. The wardrobe had clothes hooks shaped like lilies. In the living room a fencing ground was marked off with copper braid. On a shelf a yard wide, bolted to the wall, stood a collection of clay owls. Some of them were tiny; the biggest was life-size. Tristan had arranged the owls from darkest to lightest.

I had never seen such enormous windows in an apartment. The evening light canted onto the floorboards.

With his thumb, Tristan stroked the head of the squirrel in his hand.

He brought a box from a neighboring room, set it on the windowsill, and put the animal inside it.

"So," he said. "Have you ever fenced?"

He gave me a padded jacket, undressed in front of me, and put on a fencing costume. He folded his pants, hung his suit jacket on a hanger. He was pale; his muscles were long and lean.

"There's no better way to get to know somebody than in battle," he said.

"I thought the sword story was a fairy tale."

A woman appeared at the door with a white maid's cap on her head. Seeing the open box with the squirrel in it, she lowered her gaze.

"Good evening, *mademoiselle*," said Tristan. "Would you be so kind, *s'il vous plaît*, as to bring us—*nous apporter*— a . . . *pichet de bière*. And is there any Roquefort in the house?"

His French had the hard ring of the Swiss French I recognized from back home.

"Right away, Herr von Appen. Roquefort, *bien sûr.*"

The woman spoke German with a French accent.

"And, mademoiselle, there is a baby *hibou* on the windowsill. Take care that Muck does not come near it, *près de lui.*"

"*Pardon,* Monsieur von Appen. *Permettez-moi de vous corriger.*"

"Whenever you wish, *ma chère.*"

"You made a little mistake. In fact it is not an *hibou,* an owl, it is a squirrel. *Écureuil.*"

"Oh, thank you very much, *ma chère, excusez-moi, s'il vous plaît.* Thank you for telling me. Squirrel, of course, *écureuil. Merci.*"

"*Avec plaisir, cher maître.*"

With his left hand, Tristan pointed in the direction of the window toward the squirrel, outstretching his arm in the process. On his biceps I saw a small tattoo, a dark zero.

"And what would you say to a night off? They're showing *Sky Hounds* at the cinema *ce soir.*"

"Of course, Herr von Appen."

The woman left the room. Tristan said, "She's an angel. She can fold sheets with one hand. Plus, she speaks French, it's outstanding, I'm always learning."

I suited up quickly. The fencing jacket was so long that I had to roll back the cuffs. Tristan handed me an épée.

"The épée," he said. "One meter ten. I measured it. Three-cornered, flexible, made of fine Solingen steel.

He seemed to like the role of teacher.

"Originally only the nobility were permitted to own them. But there's no nobility anymore, am I right? In any case, it's the most tactical weapon in fencing."

My fingers slid over the point of the blade; it was dull.

"And also the deadliest." As he said that, Tristan pressed the tip of his épée against my chest, right above where my heart beat.

It felt strange, but on impulse, I took the weapon in my left hand. It would be easy to get my step technique wrong.

We fenced three bouts, which I lost without scoring one point. Tristan was quick; he had good reach. For a long while he fenced while singing "You're the Top," matching his strokes to the rhythm of the song. "You have it in your blood," he said after the last bout.

Afterward we ate Roquefort and drank cask beer from earthenware mugs. A drop of sweat rolled from Tristan's temple and fell into his beer stein.

"Do you like the cheese?"

I nodded.

Tristan said that in wartime it's easy to forget who we are, that the Germans are a cultured people, the nation of Heine and Wagner. He said that was why good food was so important. It was an expression of our culture. We shouldn't forget that, just because we were at war. He said, "Others see darkness. I see beauty."

He pointed to the cheese. "From the Marché des Enfants Rouges."

I saw how proud he was. "What about rationing?" I asked.

"It applies more to some than to others." He pondered. "But it's fine for you to dig in, old boy. And try the pickles from the Spree."

The housekeeper brought in preserved strawberries and sugar to sprinkle them with. Tristan spoke of Atlantis and yoga, of Madagascar and Carl Schmitt. It was no wonder that the Israelites looked so terrible, he said, given that they weren't allowed to enter hair salons anymore.

I kept on reading a sentence that was printed on the sugar bowl: "Don't be stingy with the sugar—The body needs it, sugar feeds it!"

Tristan put on a record of instrumental swing music and drummed a beat on the sugar bowl with two silver butter knives.

"I don't get this talk of Jew music," he said. "I mean, do you hear this saxophone?"

I heard it and was happy that he said that.

A glass case hung on the wall, well lit. Within it was a feather, pinned to the back of the case with a needle. I stood up and looked at the feather; it gleamed black.

"Do you know what that is?" Tristan asked.

He didn't wait for a reply.

"A chicken feather. It was given to me personally by Heinrich Himmler. From his own stock."

Tristan opened the drawer of the secretary desk that stood near the sofa and took out a revolver.

"And this, too," he said, holding the revolver in the light of the lamp. "Ever shot a man?"

He went back to the dining room. Beyond a big window facing the street stood a chestnut tree whose branches reached to the windowpanes.

"In Switzerland do you also have this war between red squirrels and gray squirrels?"

It was the first time I'd heard the term "gray squirrel." Tristan held forth at length about the stealthy gray squirrel, unknown in Europe and originating in America, which had invaded and now threatened the red squirrels. To restore the natural order, Tristan sat at the window at night and looked for gray squirrels to shoot from the tree.

"It takes me a while to get over it every time," he said, and stared outside.

He took two chairs from the table, got our coats, and for some time we sat beside each other, our feet on the windowsill, looking into the night. I saw no red squirrels or gray squirrels. If I had seen one of either kind, it would have looked gray to me anyway, but I kept that thought to myself, because I didn't want to disappoint Tristan.

He opened the cylinder of the gun, took out a bullet and gave it to me. It felt good lying in my hand: cool, smooth in front, and at the back you could trace the grooves with your fingernail.

"A memento," said Tristan.

"Thanks."

"May I ask you something?"

I nodded.

"What are you looking for here in Berlin? I mean, we're at war. You could travel anywhere. What is it that you're trying to find here?"

"The truth," I said.

"All right, okay, the truth; then what?"

"No, I mean, I came looking for the truth."

He stopped laughing. "A noble aim."

He gripped my hand and held it tight. In the other hand he held the gun.

"And you?" I asked.

"Me? What am I looking for?"

"No, have you ever shot a man?"

He looked at the revolver in his hand. Outside in the tree something rustled; I tried to ignore it.

Tristan said, "Gunpowder smells wonderful." And then he laughed.

It could have been a great night with a new friend, but I got indigestion from the pickles and left. A taxi took me back to the hotel.

I had always wished for a friend like this. I asked myself why I'd taken my sword in my bad hand and whether that had been a lie.

*

Cases #14 and #15: Frau F. and child
                                 Witnesses: 1. Frau K., 2. Elly L.

Frau F. was arrested with her child in the apartment of Aron P., who already had been deported, by the Jewish investigators B. and L. At the Grosse Hamburger Strasse camp the witnesses met Frau F., who was transported to Auschwitz with them. Frau K. was herself present when Frau F. was taken to be gassed. She stated that even though the accused was not present at the arrest of Frau F., she had scouted out the P. apartment for illegal Jewish residents.

Pp. I / 162–163
Pp. I / 16, 38, 182–184

March 1942

In the Ufa-Palast in Berlin, the film *The Great King* has its premiere. Lübeck is burning in the aftermath of a bombardment by the Royal Air Force. In the Warsaw ghetto, a young concert critic named Marcel Reich-Ranicki writes reviews for the ghetto newspaper *Gazeta Żydowska*. The third commandment of Dr. Joseph Goebbels's Ten Commandments for Every National Socialist is issued: "Each of your countrymen, even the poorest, is a part of Germany. Love him as you love yourself." To keep the German rails fully available for war transports, severe penalties are threatened for unwarranted train travel. Reinhard Heydrich orders Jews to put white paper stars on their doors to identify their apartments. In the Munich Palais, a show opens of the work of the artist Alfred Kubin. Goebbels forbids German theaters to produce the play *The Weavers*, by Gerhart Hauptmann. In the German Reich, all those who work in the fashion world are forced to become members of the Reich Chamber of Fine Arts, with the goal of making German fashion superior to French fashion. Robert Bosch, a German industrialist, engineer, and researcher, dies in Stuttgart from the consequences of an ear infection; prior to his death he had ensured that the Bosch industries would have enough forced labor to fulfill the Wehrmacht's needs.

*

In the middle of February, I had received a letter from Istanbul, in which Father asked when I was going to continue my travels and wrote that he was having good experiences with Sufism. There was a photo enclosed with the letter; on the back it said: "Choulex, 1939." The photo showed my lake behind the Minorite monastery. Father asked how I was faring under National Socialism. I drank half a bottle of cognac.

*

Case #33: G. or G.
Witness: Harry A.

Witness Harry A. was freed from political imprisonment in July and began working at the Perschner company in the Weissensee district. The accused appeared at the entrance of the workroom and, through the proprietor, Mr. P., demanded that a Jewish employee come with her. P. told the witness that the accused showed him an identity pass from the Gestapo, with the name "J." The fate of the Jew who was taken away is unknown.

Pp. I / 40, 65
Pp. I / 118, 198

*

The next morning the chambermaid woke me too early. She wanted to set out hand towels in the bathroom as she did every morning. I turned over onto my other side. My mouth was dry; my tongue stuck to the roof of my mouth.

"How beautiful it is here."

Kristin stood at the door, her feet neatly together; she was wearing high boots and surveying the books on my shelf. On her head perched a Tyrolean hat, set at an angle.

"*Perpetual Peace*, I don't know that one yet," she said, touching the spine of a book on the shelf. She took off her boots and socks and said, "I'd better tell you this right away. When I'm indoors I always have to take off my socks, otherwise I feel confined."

Kristin walked through the room, drew apart the curtains, and opened a window. I wasn't wearing a nightshirt.

"What shall we do?" she asked. She sat at the foot of the bed.

"Miss Kristin . . ."

"Kristin."

"Kristin . . . I . . . may I ask you please to turn around for a moment?"

A smile appeared on her face. "So that's the way it's going to be?"

She went to the window, pressed her fingertips against it, and looked outside.

"I won't look," she said. I could hear in her voice how much the situation amused her. I walked into the bathroom. Through the closed door I could hear her laughing.

I washed my face with cold water, chewed a little tooth-paste, and threw on a robe. I asked myself how she had managed to get into my room without telling the staff that she was my wife.

As I entered the room, Kristin was standing in front of the easel and looking at my painting efforts. She unwrapped the foil paper from one of her chocolates and leaned her pelvis against the windowsill.

"We could go to the Varieté in the Wintergarten, or to Haus Vaterland on Potsdamer Platz and hear a little jazz; Melodie Klub is still going strong. Or, do you know the Bollinger?"

She stroked the curtains.

"I bet they still have real coffee from beans here."

I called reception and ordered breakfast for us. Usually I drank only two cups of tea in the morning, but this day, because Kristin was standing beside me, I heard myself say that the waiter should bring everything they had.

That year, every adult in Germany was allotted a rationed quantity of food, soap, clothing, and coal each month. Four pounds of bread per week, 300 grams of meat, 280 grams of sugar, 206 grams of fat, 110 grams of jam, and an eighth of a pound of ersatz coffee made of chicory or malted barley. In the hotel, every waiter carried a little scissors on a chain with him for cutting off ration stubs, but guests who could pay hard cash could also eat. If you had the money the head porter would procure food on the black market. Eating didn't interest me; Kristin interested me. I paid the money.

Two employees brought chairs and a table into the room, laid out a starched cloth, and loaded it with a warm braided yeast loaf, rosehip jam, cold meat, cheese, and a basket of apples. I saw how Kristin looked at the food and smiled. Near the table the waiter set out a bucket of ice cubes and a bottle of champagne, the sight of which made me feel sick. Kristin drank two glasses and began to eat. She cut the butter thick. She ate the two soft-boiled eggs with salt and butter.

"You're a marvel," she said.

I drank tea.

"To tell the truth, I'd totally forgotten how good coffee from beans tastes," said Kristin. She balanced the cup on her leg.

I saw that she came from a simple background. My mother would have hit me with the rug beater if I'd put a cup on anything other than a saucer or filled a glass all the way to the brim.

Kristin drank and laughed and talked about how she was going to try out a new song soon and how she was going to swim with me in the Landwehr Canal in the summer. I liked listening to her.

She poured coffee into the orange juice glass, laid grilled meat on the bread, and drank from the champagne bottle.

After three-quarters of an hour she rested both hands on her stomach. I had never seen a woman eat like that, not even the cook back home.

"And now, to sleep," she said. She had drunk the bottle of champagne alone. The table was by the bed. Kristin tumbled into the rumpled sheets onto her belly.

She took a novel from the pile of books by my bed, opened the book to the middle, and started reading. She read for a while. I watched her, wondering if I should leave her alone.

"Can you get us another, please?" she asked, pointing to the champagne bucket. I realized how empty my room had been until this day.

I dressed quickly. At the bar on the ground floor the barman greeted me with the same politely indifferent smile as ever. He was called "Fat Franz." He had a waxed mustache and, despite his nickname, was lean.

I thought that everyone in the hotel must already know that a woman had come to my room this morning. I ordered a bottle of champagne. I could have called from my room, but I was so flustered that it had not occurred to me.

Fat Franz bent down. I heard the clinking of glass, then he put a bottle of champagne on the bar; the label was pearled with condensation. The barman smiled and rapped twice on the cork with the flat of his hand. "A person can't always be Goldilocks," he said, and with that he began to polish glasses. Softly he added: "Be careful, comrade."

I stopped.

"The carbonation," he said, "be careful, it doesn't suit everyone."

The double doors of my room were ajar. When I think back to that time it's the light I remember first of all. The light in Berlin is often hard and cold. Only on a few days, before spring sets in, does it shine the way it did that day. Or maybe I just want to remember it that way.

My eyes fell on the bed, on the dress and the frilly underwear that lay upon it, then on the armchair by the easel at the window. Kristin sat atop the armchair, naked, perched on the seat back. Her eyelids were heavy. She held an apple in her hand. The door slid silently shut.

"I'm not going to sleep with you," said Kristin.

She inhaled audibly.

"In school I was always the best at running. That's why my thighs are so firm."

My heart was pounding so loud that I was sure she could hear it.

"Do you want to try it?" she asked.

"Try?"

"You know, to draw the apple."

For a few moments she watched what her nakedness did to me.

"Come over here," she said.

I looked at her mouth while I walked over to her. Up on the armchair she was bigger than me. When I stood in front of her she put her hand on my neck and pulled me to her.

"You're a good boy," she said.

She started to rub her forehead against my face; she smelled like fresh bread. She reached for the champagne bottle and rested it on her thigh. Slowly she twisted the champagne's wire basket and let the cork pop. Foam dripped onto the upholstery of the armchair and left a spot.

She stroked my hand.

"You mustn't keep your fists clenched like that when you're with me," she said, grasping my fingers and opening them.

I hoped she would take me in her arms, and when she did, I knew that it was good.

"Would you call me Tink? Like Tinker Bell? I'd like that."

There was nothing I could refuse this woman. She breathed loudly and guided my hand. She was warm and soft.

"Tink," I said.

Sunbeams poured through the windows onto our skin.

*

Case #34:   von D.
   Witness: Josef von D.

As the witness Josef von D. left the Aschinger pub in Joachimsthaler Street, he was suddenly addressed by Rolf I. with the words: "Halt, we have you now, we've been looking for you for fourteen days." The accused and I. arrested the witness, brought him to the Zoo train station and from there by S-Bahn to the Grosse Hamburger Strasse camp. The witness was deported a few days later to Theresienstadt, where he was imprisoned until the end of the war.

Pp. I / 39, 200

April 1942

For illegal animal slaughter, a Berlin butcher is sentenced to death by hanging. Women in Germany are forced to work in arms factories. Roger Chapman is born. Benito Mussolini visits Adolf Hitler in Obersalzberg. Joseph Goebbels bans the hit song "Lili Marleen" when he discovers that the singer Liese-Lotte Helene Berta Wilke, known as Lale Andersen, is friends with Swiss Jews. As the official in charge of the Four-Year Plan, Hermann Göring increases the workweek for public employees to fifty-six hours. The fourth of Dr. Joseph Goebbels's Ten Commandments for Every National Socialist is issued: "Seek for yourself only duties. Then Germany will regain its rights." After attacks on the German occupying forces, all theaters and cinemas in Paris are shut down for three days. In Russia, the spring thaw comes, and, with it, the fighting there comes to an overall halt. In Belorussian Minsk, construction begins on a repair facility for military vehicles, its direction undertaken by the Daimler-Benz company. Jews are prohibited from using public transportation in the German Reich. German troops in Russia receive almost no supplies. Eight hundred Westphalian Jews from the Arnsberg region are deported. The Reichstag, in its final session, grants Adolf Hitler, as the "Supreme Authority," complete freedom in decision-making.

*

From that day on, Kristin and I spent time together. She came every morning on the tram. We ate food from the black market and watched Berlin through the hotel's latticed windows.

Kristin drank a lot, even in the mornings, but alcohol didn't change her the way it did Mother. At night, if Kristin had eaten more than three chocolates, she sometimes emptied out my wardrobe and put everything back again over and over. She folded everything her way: she turned the collars under and crossed the sleeves across the shirtfronts.

She wished I would move into a bigger room. I moved one floor higher, into a suite with a living room and a copper bathtub. "You're such a marvel," said Kristin.

I had my hotel bill sent to my father, as before. I wrote to him in a letter that I would be staying a little longer in Berlin. I ignored his question about how I was getting along with the Germans.

The new room was so big that my steps echoed on the parquet.

Kristin had told the staff that she was my fiancée. I didn't speak to her about it. The one-armed elevator operator said, "A hearty Heil Hitler to the young couple." Kristin liked the copper bathtub. She lay inside it and drank champagne from the bottle. She bathed so long that she had to run more hot water. She read the books on the bookshelf and asked me to get Hemingway's banned novels for her.

When she emerged from the foam, the skin under her little feet was rippled. Her whole body smelled of soap. I liked drying her off. Kristin hid notes among my shirts. She wrote in tiny letters.

Under my pillow one note said: "You smell good."

Once the head porter stopped me as I was leaving the hotel alone and gave me a folded note: "Will you be nice to me tonight?"

On one note, which I found in my left shoe, it said: "I'm proud of you, Fritz."

I thought she was overdoing it, but every note made me happy.

"Will you take me with you to your villa at the lake?" Kristin often asked, and ignored me when I told her the lake was just a short walk from the house.

"The important thing is the lake," she said.

The thought of taking her home appealed to me.

"Will you take me to your villa at the lake?"

"Later."

"Done."

She talked about her preference for being painted in oil ("The paint smells so good"). And how she imagined her future as a singer ("To tell the truth, I want adoring fans to shower me with a thousand gladioli"). What she did to get over a hangover ("My secret cure is pickled herring"). She said how sweet her father was when he played piano in his dressing gown, and that her mother made the best pancakes in the world. It didn't seem to bother her if I didn't talk.

She brought condoms in boxes into the hotel with her, stacked the empty boxes on the windowsill and told the chambermaid that she wasn't allowed to clear them away. Kristin liked to tell me tips she'd overheard at the art school.

"You just have to concentrate on the negative space," she said; or "Simply observe the object as an assemblage of forms, get it?" That worked on apples, although there was hardly any negative space around an apple, but it didn't work when I tried to draw her.

I asked her where she got all her chocolates and how much they cost. She said, "You're so inquisitive."

She never spent the night with me. When I asked where she lived, she shook her index finger at me scoldingly and said her mother would worry if she didn't come home at night.

How could I have been so naive?

Isn't that something you always ask yourself when you look back? One night I went after her. When she got up and left, I waited a moment then followed her. In the government district she walked with quick steps in a westward direction. She talked to every policeman she came across. She wore her fair hair loose; nobody asked her for her papers. In Tiergarten she started picking up her pace, and then she ran. I didn't understand why. I ran after her, and for a few minutes I could keep up, then I lost my breath. I watched as her silhouette disappeared between the trees.

One day as she rested her head on my stomach, Kristin asked, "What's your favorite color?"

"What do you mean?"

"Well, the color you like best of all."

"I don't have one."

"Everyone has one."

"I'm color blind."

She turned onto her side. "Red-green, is that right?"

I didn't look at her. I told her about the coachman.

Kristin stroked my hair. I could see from the little furrow between her brows that she was thinking about what I had said.

"Will the colors ever come back to you?"

"At least red, Mother always said."

"Not red, that's boring."

She sat up.

"Light green, of course."

Hand in hand, we went into the Tiergarten. She pulled me after her and we came to a stop in front of a young beech tree.

"Pay attention," she said, and, taking my hand, put a leaf between my index finger and thumb.

"Light green. Like a new morning."

"You find such good words," I said.

"Liar," she said, and hooked her fingers through the hair at the back of my neck, pulling my face to hers.

That day I showed Kristin how to suck nectar from lilac blossoms.

We kissed beneath a park sign that said: "Citizens, respect your environment. Walk your dogs on a leash," and below that, in smaller print: "The yellow benches are authorized for use by Jews, by order of the Reich Citizenship Law." All the benches were gray, she told me.

"My eyes are blue," she said, "can you see that?"

"I would have guessed green," I said.

*

Case #17: R.
Witness: Paul R.

The witness Paul R. was addressed by the accused on the Kurfürstendamm at Joachimsthaler Street. She told him that she had too little to eat and hardly anything to wear. R., who did not know of her activities, assumed she was an illegal resident. On her initiative, they both went into the Klausner restaurant. The accused left the witness, supposedly to make a phone call. When she returned to the table, R. said ironically, "So, did you call your boyfriend?" upon which the accused responded, "No, not this time." Some ten minutes later, the accused stood up again and left the table, at which point several members of the Gestapo suddenly entered, among them the camp director Dobberke. R. was delivered to the camp on Grosse Hamburger Strasse. During transport to Auschwitz he managed to escape from the boxcar.

Pp. I / 40, 165

*

Spring came. I went more often to the art school. The number of students dropped.

"Where have they all gone?" I asked the secretary with the smeared glasses.

"They've taken the train to Lisbon."

"What for?"

"Are you joking?"

"No."

"For safety's sake, you idiot."

"Are you afraid, too?" I asked.

The woman snorted. "Fear, fear, war, peace. Everyone keeps talking all the time about the Final Victory, about the war, the Jews, the Slavs, and the Final Victory. It's all meaningless. What you should ask is when there will be decent soap in the shops again."

Kristin and I walked with Tristan in the park, sat on a blanket, and ate nougat candy that Tristan took from a white cardboard box. "From Montélimar," he said softly.

On the way home, Kristin, Tristan, and I held hands.

"Heil there," said Tristan, when a policeman passed by. We laughed at this German Volk and this war. There were no moving trucks to be seen.

All three of us went to the Melodie Klub. Tristan greeted every soldier along the way. Sometimes he winked at me. He introduced me to the barmaid with the freckles and showed me a couple of dance steps.

One time Tristan came to the hotel with a bicycle, pushing a second bicycle with him, which he had brought all the way from Savignyplatz. In greeting, he said, "The sun shines bright up in the sky, the crablouse scurries down my thigh." He gave me the bike with the crossbar and took the ladies' bike for himself.

"Muck has to run," he said. "They're made for running, these greyhoundiños."

The dog ran along behind us, his ears fluttering. Tristan rode with no hands, laughed a little to himself, and then loudly sang a song.

> *When the storm trooper faces the fire,*
> *It fills him with delight.*

Our faces were warm with the spring sun. Tristan laughed at me.

"Watch the road instead," I said.

"What could happen to us?" he called into the wind.

When Tristan brought me back to the hotel that night and embraced me and said goodbye, he said, "They have to run. It's their nature, you understand? They run. And if they don't run, they die."

Tristan invited Kristin and me to a garden party, on Schwanen-werder island, at the lake in Wannsee. It was the garden party of one of the Reich ministries.

"There'll be venison. Will you come?"

I didn't want to go to any party given by a National Socialist ministry. I wondered how he happened to be on the guest list.

"No thanks, Tristan."

He turned to Kristin. "And you, little girl?"

She snuggled up against me, her chest on my upper arm. "Oh, come on, dear Friedrich, let's go," she said.

Tristan winked at me.

I asked what I should bring as a gift. Tristan said that nobody in the Ministry of Public Enlightenment needed gifts.

For the party I had my evening clothes sent from Choulex. The cook and a few gardeners still lived there. On the telephone, the cook said she'd wondered how I was able to leave the hotel after six o'clock without a dinner jacket.

Kristin tried on a dark silk dress that I thought seemed too somber for her. She had spotted it in the window of a little boutique on Unter den Linden. The saleswoman said it was from Paris, made by Coco Chanel.

"Will you buy it for me?" Kristin asked.

"Are you sure?"

She shrugged her shoulders. "I was just kidding. I've got prettier ones."

The day before the garden party there was an air-raid warning. Because the wail of the siren didn't reach into the hotel, a page banged a gong when the alarm went off and walked through the hall, repeatedly striking it. I will never forget that sound.

When there were air-raid alerts, all hotel guests were required to descend into a steel-clad underground bunker. The staff stayed in a boiler room. Guests had access to passageways under Pariser Platz that led to a room with a ventilation system that apparently would still function in the event of a direct hit on the hotel.

In the underground bunker, the men played cards and Fat Franz served red wine and chocolate. There were gas masks under the chairs. Kristin sat beside me in the bunker, beamed at me, and drank wine. "Definitely just a test," she said. Sometimes a fiddler played down below.

When the gong sounded early in the evening on the day before the garden party, Kristin and I were in bed.

"The gong," I said, and took a breath.

"Not yet," said Kristin.

"But the gong." I thought of the gas masks under the chairs in the bunker. Once someone had called them "Volksgasmasks."

"Keep going," said Kristin.

We stayed in bed, and the gong fell silent. The streetlights were out; every neon sign, every light in every apartment, was turned off. Berlin was shrouded in darkness so the bombers would not be able to orient themselves. I stood up and looked outside. The street was empty. Berlin was dark.

"What should we do now?" I asked. Through the window I could see the stars.

Kristin looked at me and grinned. "Go to the bunker."

We got dressed and walked downstairs hand in hand. Kristin took her coat with her, but I noticed that only later. The door to the cellar was locked. I rattled the knob.

"I know of another bunker, come on." Kristin dragged me after her through the lobby.

Berlin lay quiet before us. Kristin went ahead of me on the sidewalk; she skipped and stretched out a hand behind her without looking back at me. I took her hand. Kristin went faster than me and pulled me along with her. Then she turned around and smiled. After a couple meters, I realized we weren't going to any bunker.

I looked up into the sky. "Where are you going?"

"For a walk."

"But that's dangerous."

"It doesn't matter."

At the corner of Friedrichstrasse, at an air defense position, we heard the laughter of soldiers behind sandbags. That reassured me. There was nobody on the street but us.

"Look," said Kristin. The dark silk dress she had tried on two days earlier was on a mannequin in the display window. Kristin gripped the knob of the locked shop door.

At home in Choulex we had a toolshed with a sticky door lock, and one of our gardeners had shown me how to open the door with a knife.

"I could break in," I said.

"Show me," said Kristin.

I looked at her dimples. I knew what she was thinking. She was thinking I would do anything for her. I took my folding knife out of my pocket. Kristin giggled. Without a sound, I opened the blade and, in one movement, slipped it into a crack and opened the door of the boutique. I took the dress and gave it to Kristin. She stuffed it into her coat pocket.

"You darling, marvelous man," she said. "Thank you."

On the Weidendammer Bridge we sat on the railings.

"Fontane got engaged on this bridge," said Kristin, and after a bit: "By the way, I'm terrified of heights."

I unbuttoned my shirt and let it fall behind me on the footpath. As I took off my trousers, I almost lost my balance. The steel of the bridge felt cold against my thighs. I kept my hat on. I jumped, made a three-quarter turn, and landed with a smack on my bare back on the surface of the water. Kristin leaned out over the railings. The water tasted of diesel. As I climbed up a ladder on the riverbank, my hat between my teeth, Kristin came running and dried me off with her coat.

"You really are something," she said. I don't know if she sounded impressed or if she was laughing at me.

We went hand in hand back to the hotel, slowly, because it was beautiful out. From time to time I looked at her out of the corner of my eye, and once I caught her looking at me, too. No bombs fell on Berlin that night.

The next morning I sent a messenger to the boutique to drop off an anonymous envelope with money in it.

The day of the party, Kristin arrived at the hotel at midday, bathed with lavender oil, let her hair air-dry, and sat on a stool in front of the vanity mirror. I thought she was more beautiful without makeup, the way she came to me in the mornings, when she arrived without having washed.

She pushed me away. "You're messing up my hair."

She plucked her eyebrows and applied rouge, dark kohl, and a pale lipstick. I think she overdid it because I was sitting on the edge of the bathtub watching her and because makeup back then was considered an American thing, a little indecent.

She twisted her hair into a bun. Kristin was taking a long time, we would get there late; it didn't bother me. She was reading *All Quiet on the Western Front*, by Erich Maria

Remarque, who once had been her neighbor in Wilmersdorf, as she liked to say. She lay down in bed on her stomach.

"Shall we go, Tink?"

"Right away."

I leaned against the door and gazed at Kristin—that was enough for me.

Before we left the room, she took the flask of my cologne. Father had given it to me. I used it rarely. Its fragrance smelled of bay leaves and, a little, of rum. Kristin sprayed the perfume over her head and looked up.

"It's for men," I said.

"Everything always smells sweet on me anyway." She leaned her pelvis against me. "I'd like so much to go to the party by carriage."

"It's too far."

"I think it would be nice."

The carriage trip lasted almost two hours. Kristin held my fingers. I felt the pulse in her wrist. She stroked the satin stripe of my trousers.

The villa was built of bricks, with sandstone columns in front. The drive was covered with gravel and lined with cherry trees in bloom. Kristin unwrapped two of her chocolates from their tinfoil, chewed them, gave me the empty wrappers, and hooked her arm through mine. We walked up the narrow path to the entrance.

"I'm a little nervous, to tell the truth," she whispered. "Do I have chocolate between my teeth?"

Many men were wearing uniforms and swastika armbands; others were in dinner jackets. Kristin didn't look nervous.

Tristan came to us with two full glasses; he greeted Kristin with a kiss on the hand and me with an embrace. He wore a tailored double-breasted dinner jacket, his hair was parted, and in his buttonhole there was a dark badge, on which two lightning bolts could be seen. Tristan von Appen, my friend, was in the Schutzstaffel.

A band played music that reminded me of a polka.

Kristin pulled me across the parquet through the rooms of the villa's ground floor until we reached the buffet. Slices of hardboiled eggs with trout caviar and thin cuts of venison. You could have forgotten we were living in wartime.

Kristin loaded eggs on her plate, went to the terrace, leaned against a wall, and ate with her fingers. She said, "All the men are looking, but I don't want them. I am your woman now."

"Did you see that Tristan has an SS pin?"

"Yes."

I looked at her. She licked her fingertips clean.

"So?" she asked.

A path lined with torches led to the water. I walked down it alone, sat on the wall of the quay, and looked at the lights of the villas on the opposite shore. Every light seemed to me like a promise. I turned around and watched the revelers from afar. Kristin stood alone; I trusted her.

Tristan came down the path and sat beside me.

"How are you feeling?" he asked.

I didn't reply.

"Boring, isn't it?"

I nodded. "Are you with the SS, Tristan?"

"Obersturmbannführer, old boy, it's simply the best uniform." He winked.

"Do you really mean that?" I asked.

"Half."

"What does that mean?"

"You two are an item, right?"

"Yes, but wait a second, you like Benny Goodman and all that."

He looked out over the lake.

"Do we have to discuss this tonight?" asked Tristan softly, and then, loudly, "Do you think you'll have children? Little Kristin and you? I want to have five."

He put his arm around me.

"Where does our little Kristin work, actually?"

I didn't know. "She teaches Latin somewhere, Tristan, I—"

"Latin? Kristin?"

"I don't really know."

"Should I find a job for her? She could be a typist in one of the ministries. I've already spoken about it with one of the directors. Latin . . . are you certain?"

I didn't want my friend Tristan to be in the SS. I didn't want Kristin to work for a Reich ministry. I wanted the three of us to dance some more.

"No," I said.

Tristan smiled. "What is our little dove's last name?"

A shout interrupted us. Up at the top of the path stood a wiry, short man in uniform. "Von Appen!" he bellowed.

Tristan threw his empty glass into the lake and turned to go.

"Tristan," I said.

He turned around. "Old boy?"

"I want to know what you do for the SS."

"I'm an Obersturmbannführer."

"But what do you do?"

He came up to me and put his hands on my shoulders. "Another time, my friend, I promise."

He kissed me on the forehead and sprang up the path, taking long, fast strides. When he was halfway up the path, the man at the top shouted again, "Von Appen!" though he could see that Tristan was on the way. Tristan was more than a head taller when he stood before him. Tristan saluted him. Every aspect of his demeanor was as it should be.

The glass that he had thrown in the water floated for a moment then went under.

Kristin was still leaning against the wall; she'd wrapped her arms around her body and her hands lay on her shoulders, probably to warm herself. Cold air rose from the water. A man stood beside Kristin; he had a friendly face and a narrow upper lip, and his dinner jacket was tight across his belly. I was relieved that he wore no uniform or swastika armband. Kristin smiled when she saw me and beckoned to me.

"I can't believe it," she said, "this is Ernst Hiemer."

She laid her finger on the man's arm. I nodded. Kristin gripped my hand. Her grip was too tight.

"Ernst Hiemer, the famous children's book author. *The Poisonous Mushroom*, Fritz. Such a wonderful book."

I didn't know the book. Hiemer's handshake was warm and pleasant.

Kristin took two glasses of champagne from a waiter's tray and drank one of them immediately. She drew my arm around her shoulders, so that my elbow hooked around her neck.

"How does the preface go again? Truth to tell, it's always given me goose bumps," she said.

Hiemer blushed. Kristin was masterful. She had him.

"You're embarrassing me, young lady. You really want to hear it?"

"Yes. Please." Kristin held me tight or I held her, it was hard to say.

"Since it's for you, my lady."

Hiemer sighed, glanced at me, and took a breath. He looked as if it was a little uncomfortable for him, but he spoke with the voice of a storyteller and paused for effect between the sentences. He knew the preface by heart.

"Germans must learn to recognize the poisonous mushroom. They must recognize the danger that the Jew presents to the German people and to the entire world. They must learn that the Jewish Question affects us all. The following stories tell us the truth about the poisonous Jewish mushroom." His voice reminded me of Father's.

"They show us the many forms that the Jew can assume." He paused and looked at us individually. "They show us the depravity and baseness of the Jewish race. They show us what the Jew truly is . . ."

He smiled, raised a finger, and glanced expectantly at Kristin. She had been listening to him with her mouth slightly parted, and said softly, "The Devil in human form."

"Bravo," said Hiemer, and grasped her hand. "So, enough of that. I hope that you dance?"

"Dance?" she asked.

"A little polka."

"Gladly."

"May I?" asked Hiemer, looking at me.

I said nothing. He smiled with an open mouth. I wondered if I had ever seen a man with such straight teeth. Kristin leaned against me.

"Friedrich, just one dance?"

"Why do you know your own preface by heart?" I asked.

Hiemer smiled. Kristin squeezed my hand.

"Of course, go dance," I said, kissed her cheek, and nodded to Hiemer. "Be my guest."

Through the window of the ballroom I watched as the two of them danced a waltz, then walked to the lake and threw up over the quay wall.

I sat for a long time on the cold stone. I looked out on the water and only noticed her when she put her arms around me from behind. A couple of strands of hair had come loose from her bun and fell in her face. Her kohl had run. Her body exuded heat.

"This Hiemer, such a little manikin, he dances better than you'd think. And he was quite skillful at flirting."

"Do you really believe that?"

"What?"

"'The Devil in human form.'"

She kissed me, ignoring the fact that I smelled of vomit. "Naturally," she said, and flicked me on the nose with her finger.

"But why?"

"Because everyone says it, you dreamer," she said, holding my neck and looking me in the face for a long moment. "Look in your left inside pocket."

I pulled out a note. On it was written in her neat handwriting, "Kiss me."

She had taken on a hard look; her eyelids were half closed. Her lashes were long. "Come over here," she said.

"This is all garbage," I said. I pushed her away and shook my head. "All these lies. These stories of poisonous mushrooms. You can't really believe that. I mean, you gave the woman in the tram your coffee."

"For God's sake, Friedrich, don't be so tiresome."

She grabbed my arm. I pulled her to me.

"At home, the lake, the one I told you about."

"The lake," said Kristin mildly.

"There's a stone wall there. It's very high. Once I jumped from it."

She shook her head and smiled. "Truly," she said, "I've never met anyone like you."

She took me back to the party. The band had stopped playing; the musicians were packing up their instruments. Kristin drank a full glass of cherry brandy and called out into the ballroom, "A song, a song."

Soon the revelers began to sing. I didn't want to drink anymore. I didn't know most of the tunes. As it grew late, Tristan and his superiors sang the song he'd sung earlier, on the bicycle. This time I heard the whole refrain.

> *When the storm trooper faces the fire,*
> *It fills him with delight.*
> *And when Jews' blood streams from the knife,*
> *Then everything is right.*

The people sang loudly and well; there were a lot of basses, and among them I heard Kristin's faint soprano. She had hooked her arm through Tristan's. Her chest swelled when she drew breath. I felt a tremor of disgust; I gripped the note in my pants pocket. When our eyes met, Kristin smiled.

On the ride back, the streets looked misty in the light of the head-lamps. Kristin slept on my lap. For a long time no car passed from the opposite direction; the forest was dark around us.

I thought about Tristan. I had become friends, it seemed, with a man who was in the SS. I had no idea what he'd done as a soldier. I had fenced with him, drunk champagne with him. I remembered his salute. Did I want a friend like that?

I looked down at Kristin's face, remembered her sing-ing those vile songs and dancing with that loathsome Ernst Hiemer. I thought about how happy she had looked, standing under that Swastika flag.

"Fritz?" she whispered.

"I'm right here."

I carried Kristin from the car into our room. In the bath-room I washed her face and gave her a glass of water to drink. A couple of drops ran down her chin and onto her throat.

I stripped off her dark silk dress, hung it up, and dressed her in one of my nightshirts. It was the first night that she stayed over with me. She grasped my left forefinger with her hand and held it in her fist.

I watched her, afraid, and tried not to fall asleep. Once I laid my head on her breast to check to see if she was still breathing. I thought about how good it would be if we were the only people in the world, away from all this.

In the morning, before the sun rose, I heard her get up and go into the bathroom. She dressed in the dark. I pretended I was asleep when she left the room.

*

Case #32:   *Various Unknown Persons*
            Witness: Robert Z.

The witness Robert Z. observed many occasions when the accused, to some extent in cooperation with her husband, carried out raids on Jews on the Kurfürstendamm. Both then arranged for the identified persons to be loaded onto waiting trucks and taken away. In one raid, on the corner of Leibnizstrasse, the accused advised the witness to leave the area. A short time afterward, the witness saw an open truck drive by in which various people sat, including, at the back of the vehicle, the accused and Rolf I. The fate of the persons apprehended is not known.

Pp. I / 113R, 195

May 1942

Mexico declares war on Germany. In a radio address, the British Prime Minister Winston Churchill warns the German army against the use of poison gas. The fifth of Dr. Joseph Goebbels's Ten Commandments for Every National Socialist is issued: "Be proud of Germany. You should take pride in a Fatherland for which millions gave their lives." The British foreign minister Robert Anthony Eden and his official Soviet counterpart, Vyacheslav M. Molotov, sign a treaty against the German Reich. In New York Bing Crosby and other musicians record the song "White Christmas." The monthly ration of fat is reduced from 1,053 to 825 grams. Goebbels proclaims a politeness campaign in Berlin. Under "Operation Ironclad," British soldiers occupy Madagascar. Two Czechs in the service of the Czechoslovakian government-in-exile attempt to assassinate the acting Reich Protector, Reinhard Heydrich, in his Mercedes Cabriolet at a hairpin curve in Prague. One of the assassins fires at Heydrich with an automatic pistol, which fails because the firearm is jammed. Another assassin throws a hand grenade, which ricochets off the right back wheel of the automobile and then detonates. The force of the explosion shatters one of Heydrich's ribs and ruptures his diaphragm. Splinters of metal penetrate his spleen. Heydrich survives for the moment.

*

She didn't come back, not in the evening, not the next day.

I asked myself what I'd done wrong and thought it must have had something to do with our conversation at Wannsee.

I sat silently at the bar in the lobby and thought about her. "Your fiancée?" Fat Franz asked after a couple of days of silence.

I nodded.

At night, when no other guests were sitting at the bar, the head porter would sit beside me. He looked tired; a lock of hair drooped onto his forehead. Franz put three shot glasses on the marble, filled to the rim with corn liquor. The porter put his hand on my shoulder and said, "Nothing helps, my son."

"I can't bear it."

"Oh, sure you can, we all have to bear it, somehow."

I now had no reason to wash the charcoal dust off my hands at night.

I knew I'd made a mistake, but I didn't know how. I missed the scent of her that clung to the sheets for the first days then disappeared. I missed calling her Tink.

In my coat collar I found a strand of her fair hair. For half a day I mulled what to do with it before plucking it off the cloth. I put it in my mouth and washed it down with cognac.

I imagined her coming through the revolving door of the hotel, skipping the way she did when she was happy.

The chambermaids put lilies on my windowsill and brought me hot chocolate, which I poured down the sink.

I sent the identical telegram to Father in Istanbul and Mother in Munich:

Still in Berlin. In love. Unhappy.

Mother wrote in her letter:

Dear Fritz,

I told you long ago not to go to Berlin. And I can't be terribly moved by your unhappiness when I consider all the souls who are fighting for the Fatherland and for us, so many of whom must sacrifice their lives in the fight against the terrorists.

That's the only thing that we must pay attention to and give our support to now. Personal sorrow is an individual concern that should be forgotten.

Come to Munich, to me. I will be there, and you will see how beautiful it is here in Nymphenburg.

I greet you with Heil Hitler,
Your mother

Father wrote in his letter:

My dear son!

It warms my heart to hear from you. Imagine where I'm sitting right now. A little coffeehouse on the Bosporus, the waiter speaks French with a strong Ottoman accent; I am drinking black coffee, you can't imagine how strong it is. It's called mokka, and it's brewed with cardamom. Doesn't it sound delicious? Something an exotic Moor out of One Thousand and One Nights would drink! It is prepared in a little pot, called an ibrik, if I've understood correctly. The grind is as finely milled as sand, and it's boiled together with water, a devil's brew, as you can imagine! The waiter told me that in the past the Bedouins used to heat their coffeepots in the hot sand of the desert or on the coals of their fires. Yes, Friedrich, I'm so close to the Sahara here, you would be jealous! How great would it be if you could be here? But, by my reading, you're as in love with the wicked city of Berlin as I am besotted by old Constantinople. I know that feeling of connection to the unknown. We Bedouins only feel at home when we're on the move. And you must not feel sad—your homeland will remain a compass for you, always pointing in the right direction. But the question of when to go is up to you. I will tell you a little secret, which your mother must not hear. There is a high tower here with a crescent moon on the top, where every night a man sings to call the people to prayer, it wakes me up every time. Tonight, though, I have a plan. I am going to borrow our house servant's prayer jacket, walk out of the house looking all pious, and go with the Muslims to bow toward Mecca! Imagine, my son, your *father is visiting a mosque. Have you ever imagined such a thing? I must go now but will write again soon.*

With my full heart,
Your ever-loving father

PS: Sorry about the coffee stains.
PPS: I don't want to presume, but in case I misunderstood your news (which, as I say, I do not presume) and you really were talking about a woman, then take care. The women in Berlin are, according to all that one hears, reliably unreliable.

One night I went to Tristan's apartment on Savignyplatz. If he knew her last name, I might be able to find her. He came to the door in his nightshirt and, with his revolver in one hand, embraced me, holding me close.

"Old boy," he said a couple times.

The greyhound came running out of the living room and jumped up on me. Dog spit left streaks on my sleeve.

Tristan called for the housekeeper and asked her to make us a pot of tea. "The good kind with the Greek mountain herbs, yes?"

When we were alone, I said, "Kristin is gone."

Tristan nodded. "Sometimes we deceive ourselves."

"What?"

"Maybe she wasn't the way we saw her."

"What did you want to see?"

I wondered why he had received the news of her disappearance with no emotion. I spoke too loudly, Tristan patted my hand. The hair on his chest was light-colored.

"Never mind. I'm just afraid. We're all afraid."

It made me uncomfortable, the way he touched me. We drank the tea silently. The porcelain was so thin that I thought it might break in my fingers. Tristan asked me if I could stay for dinner and said that he had recently stopped eating meat. Humanity had first begun eating the flesh of animals when cavemen paired off with the Jewish cannibals.

"What are you talking about?" I asked. I looked at the dark zero on his upper arm.

"I read it in Wagner," said Tristan.

"Did you ask her about her last name?"

"And Gandhi also eats no meat. Do you know about Gandhi?"

I grabbed his arm. "Her name."

"Oh, that's why you're here." He topped up the tea and kept silent.

"Did you ask her, Tristan?"

"Yes."

"And?"

"She lied."

I smacked the table so hard that the cups shook.

"She lied about everything," said Tristan.

I stood up and left. At the door Tristan caught up with me and grabbed my shoulder. He spoke too calmly.

"I know that you're no Israelite," he said, "don't worry, I checked that out a long time ago. You certainly look like one, but you're clean."

We will get through this. My father had spoken that sentence. Every day in Germany I had been going through this, acting as if I could live with what was happening to the Jews in Germany. I had put up with the flags with swastikas and with the people greeting me and roaring at me with their right arms outstretched. At this moment, I felt how wrong this was. I thought about Father and the cook and I felt ashamed.

Without looking back, I ran out of the apartment. I ran until sweat was pouring off my back, down my shirt. In Mommsenstrasse I sat down on the marble steps of the entrance to a house. A couple was passing, an old man and old woman who were holding hands, their fingers interlaced.

Kristin came eight days after the night at Schwanenwerder. She knocked so faintly on my door that at first I didn't hear her. When I looked Kristin in the face, I said, "My God."

Her cheeks were sunken; she had a scarf wrapped around her head. She had bruises under both eyes. One of her eyeballs was also dark—blood had seeped into the vitreous body. It was a warm day. She was wearing a coat. She didn't touch me. In the room we stayed standing in front of one another.

"No kiss?" she asked.

When I put my arm on her she flinched. She smelled of blood.

"I wasn't careful enough," she said softly. I could hardly understand her.

"What happened?"

When she raised her arm, I saw her face contort in pain. She put her hand on my mouth.

"I thought you'd left me," I said.

"Help me out of my coat, Fritz. My shoulders . . ."

I saw the welts on her arms. As I lifted her coat up, the belt caught on her scarf, which slipped off her head. For a moment I stopped breathing. Her hair had been shaved off. She had dark welts on her neck. I could see her scalp. Kristin turned away.

"I wasn't careful enough," she said again. "Not careful enough." She sobbed, balled up her fist, and pounded herself on the forehead.

"What happened?"

She coughed, and I saw how much it hurt her. She said it would be easier for her if she didn't have to look at me while she told her story.

She turned a chair toward the window and looked outside as she spoke. It took a long time. Every now and then she fell silent; once she shouted, but otherwise she spoke calmly.

"They said I was a Jew," she began.

Kristin told me that she was the daughter of Berlin Jews. Three-day Jews, she said, because they went to the synagogue in Wilmersdorf only on three holidays a year. Her father had fought against the French in the First World War and was a member of the Reich Federation of Jewish Front-Line Soldiers. In her room on Xantener Street there was a bureau with a drawer full of his medals. He was a composer with a passion for German lieder, especially Schubert and Schumann. The family was poor.

Everything—Kristin pointed to the room where we were sitting—was like a dream to her. The food was so good, the duvet so soft. She had never drunk champagne before she met me.

She was not a Jew, she said. She didn't look like a Jew, had no Jewish friends, spoke no Yiddish, unlike the Jews from the east. She did not believe in God.

"I'm purely Aryan," she said.

She ate bacon. She didn't know the evening prayer by heart. It was Hitler who had made her a Jew.

Night after night, while synagogues burned in Fasanenstrasse and firemen stood in front and watched, Kristin had kept secret the fact that the red letter "J" was printed on her identity card. She wanted to be a singer, a profession that was forbidden to Jews. Her parents had no money for the trip to America. She had believed that Germany would spare her because her father had fought in the war and because a people that loved Schubert couldn't be entirely wicked.

Kristin's life had been fine, with her meager earnings from the art school and the Latin lessons and her performances at the Melodie Klub. She and her parents slept in an illegal lodging house.

Two days after the party at Schwanenwerder, men in leather coats came and arrested her and her parents. The men told them to get dressed, that they would be back home in a couple hours, and took them to the Jewish Affairs office on Burgstrasse. Who had informed on them, Kristin didn't know.

With a straight razor, a man shaved off the hair on her head, under her arms, and between her legs, without using any soap. He said her blood stank of sow. She had to stay overnight in a basement room where the water was ankle-deep. It was hard to sleep there; the water smelled of mold. Luckily it was late spring, she said, otherwise it would have been cold.

In the daytime she was led to a windowless room, which the men called "the office." One man there called himself "the gardener"; he sat on a chair and smoked. On the walls were photographs of flowers torn from the pages of a calendar.

The gardener had red hair that fell in long curls. A naked lightbulb hung from the ceiling, shedding a bluish light. Kristin's hands were shackled behind her back. A hook dangled from a forged chain.

The gardener brought his shirts with him to the office. He put up an ironing board in the cellar. He filled an iron with coal, unlocked Kristin's shackles, and let her iron his shirts. He praised her for getting the wrinkles out of the cotton even in the tricky places, like the shoulder seams and the collar.

The gardener slung Kristin's shackles over the hook that hung from the ceiling and used a winch to raise her about half a meter off the floor. For a few seconds her shoulder muscles were strong enough to carry the weight of her body, then her shoulders came out of the sockets and she hung limp with outstretched arms. The gardener hit her with a rubber hose. He clicked his tongue between blows. The gardener spoke a Bavarian dialect. He said, "Let's say there's a stable full of Lipizzaner horsies or something of that ilk, and somehow by accident, in every generation, a Belgian plow horse gets into the mix. The genetic ability for running will decline, while the genetic ability to pull a carriage through the mud will shoot through the roof. But then, that's a whole other quality, you know. It's the same way with people."

The gardener wanted to know where the Jewish forger Cioma Schönhaus was hiding. Kristin didn't know. Schönhaus was accused of forging documents with the help of a swastika stamp and Pelikan erasing liquid.

Kristin named addresses that seemed plausible to her. She admitted to being a race defiler. She hoped the gardener would beat her unconscious.

The blows with the hose were not the worst part. Afterward she lay on the floor with her dislocated arms.

"They ripped me apart," she said.

Several times the gardener dropped an Olivetti typewriter on her, even though it damaged the typewriter. Kristin had to pick up the machine from the floor and put it back on the table, so the gardener could throw it at her again.

If he found a wrinkle in his shirt, he threw the iron.

After a couple of days, he relocated her arms, and other men gave her a head scarf and drove her in a closed car to Wilmersdorf. The men said that if she wanted to see her parents alive again she would have to find out where the forger Cioma Schönhaus was staying. Otherwise the train would leave soon, with her parents on it. The gardener had said, "God be with you," Bavarian style, in parting.

"What should I do now, Friedrich?"

"But you never wore a star."

"I had false papers."

"That's why you never took me home with you."

"Oh, Friedrich."

She turned on her chair to face me. Tears had formed salt crystals in the corners of her eyes. There was a hardness in her face that I'd never seen before in her. Her pale skin no longer caught the light.

"My Kristin," I said.

"Friedrich," she said, "Kristin is not my real name." She looked at me. "It's Stella. Stella Goldschlag.

"What do we do now?" she asked.

She sat in my lap. I saw her grimace from pain.

"I'll call you a doctor, Kristin."

"Stella," she said, and looked past me.

"I'll call you a doctor."

The head porter asked no questions. He said a doctor would come as soon as possible.

Scarcely an hour later a man entered our suite, carrying a leather case. Instead of a white coat, he wore a tweed suit.

"What month are we in then, miss?" he asked, before he looked at Stella, and then, once he had: "Forgive me please." He did not ask how she had gotten her injuries. Throughout the examination I remained in the room. The doctor carefully felt Stella's shoulders.

"The joint on the left has been put back in place incorrectly, I need to reset it," he said. He took out a syringe and gave her a shot of a clear liquid in the crook of her arm.

"Please bring me a towel," said the doctor.

I went to the bathroom and came back with a stack of towels. He gave one of them to Stella. The shoulder joint cracked as he first dislocated and then relocated it. Stella scrunched her eyes; her teeth bit down on the towel.

Afterward the doctor dabbed one of her welts with iodine.

"Would you leave us alone for a moment?" he asked.

"He stays," said Stella.

She lay down on the bed, and the doctor lifted her dress high up on her stomach and examined her. I stayed in my armchair. I did not know what the doctor was doing, but I saw the thread he was sewing with. Stella looked at me while he was doing it; sometimes her eyelids fluttered. I maintained eye contact, to convince her that everything was going to be all right. Maybe I should have felt rage at the men who hurt Stella, at the Germans who felt entitled to throw a typewriter at a human being. But what I felt was fear—a fear that invaded every part of me. Fear of what would happen if they came back to get Stella. Of whether I could lose her again. Of what was to come.

I paid the doctor and gave him a hundred Reichsmarks to buy his silence.

When we were alone, Stella asked again, "What do we do now?"

I sat beside her in bed for a long time, holding her hand.

"Let's go to Choulex," I said.

"I can't."

"Then let's take the Orient Express and just get away from here."

"But my parents."

Her tears flowed silently. Wiping them away didn't help.

At that moment, I decided I would stay by her side. It didn't matter what her name was. She was the woman who wrote me little notes. She had no choice.

"I know who can help us," I said.

Stella raised her head. I took a breath before I said it.

Tristan called me that very day in the hotel to invite me to dinner. I knew that the invitation was no accident.

When he opened the door of his apartment two days later and saw Stella beside me, he raised his eyebrows high. Tristan was wearing a bathrobe with the insignia of the SS on the breast.

"You shouldn't have brought her here," he said, as the door swung shut.

On the dining table, fine cheeses were heaped in bowls of painted porcelain and on metal trays.

"Will you just take a look at these delicacies?" said Tristan. "It wasn't easy."

"They had me in Burgstrasse for six days," said Stella, and reached for a knife.

"Come, I'll have the table set for three. There's nothing better suited to dinner conversation."

"My parents are still down there," Stella said.

I couldn't read Tristan's expression. Stella pressed the tip of the knife against her palm. Then she pulled the scarf off her head. For a moment the tone of Tristan's voice changed; it was too high, as it often was, and now it broke at the end of the sentence: "You look terrible, young lady." He looked out the window. "What did they do to you? I mean . . . your hair?"

Stella took the knife again and pressed the tip of the blade against her hand, leaving a white mark on her skin where the blood had been pushed back.

"You have to help us," said Stella.

Tristan leaned back in his chair. He spoke even more softly than she did. "There is absolutely nothing that I have to do."

I saw Stella's hand close on the handle of the knife. Before she could move, I put my hand on hers and held it firmly. It was the first time I spoke that night.

"What can we do?"

Tristan poked for a pickle with a long steel skewer, raised it to his mouth, and chewed thoroughly. His pupils darted back and forth between us, as if he were hunting for the right words. "Friedrich, we are friends. Have you ever thought about how often she has lied to you?"

He paused for a moment and looked at the empty windowsill.

"Do you remember the little squirrel? The one I nursed back to health. Do you remember?"

He looked at Stella and focused on her.

"Let's say this apartment here is something like a kingdom. The squirrel was a guest here, yes? But the ruler of the kingdom is Muck."

The greyhound, who was lying in a corner, raised his head.

"What?" I said.

"Muck sticks his muzzle in the shoebox a couple times, but he leaves the guest in peace. Then Mademoiselle Lechaux notices that, after a couple of days, the squirrel starts crawling about. She opens a window so it can scamper back to someplace like its own kingdom, or somewhere else, it doesn't matter where; the important thing is, away."

"Tristan, what's your point?"

"It doesn't scamper out. It stays in the apartment, where there are hazelnuts that others gather for it. And bit by bit—sorry, Kristin—its Jewified character shows itself."

"Tristan, stop."

He stood up, the skewer in his hand, and positioned himself at the window with his back to us. He spoke without turning.

"Then the corrupt nature of its soul begins to show itself. It wants the apartment for itself alone. It doesn't matter to the squirrel that Muck was there before him. One day, Mademoiselle Lechaux will see the squirrel crawl out of his box and bite Muck on the paw, just like that."

"Stop, Tristan."

"Just like that."

Stella covered her ears. Tristan kept talking.

"The squirrel was of such base character that even now it makes my hair stand on end. Muck was astonished at first. I mean, you know him. But once Muck understood, he lunged for it. Thank god he didn't eat the thing. Mademoiselle Lechaux had to get rid of it. You should have seen her when she told me about it. Totally distraught, the poor thing."

I stood up. Stella still had her hands over her ears. Tristan turned around and looked alternately at both of us. He took the skewer that he had used earlier for the pickle and pointed with it. He came toward us.

"There sits another such intruder . . ." he said.

"Tristan, drop it."

". . . and if we did not let the Mucks of Burgstrasse do their work, we would do ourselves harm."

"Stop!" I was shouting now.

He dropped the skewer on the table by Stella, placed a forefinger under her chin, and spoke so softly that I could hardly make it out. "She will hack us to pieces, along with the rest of the Israelite vermin."

I grabbed his arm. "Have you gone crazy? What the hell is wrong with you?"

I had grasped his arm in the spot where the zero was tattooed on his skin.

He dropped his finger from Stella's chin, went around the table, and sat down on his chair. His bathrobe had opened, exposing his lean chest. Tristan patted his lips with the napkin.

"Tristan," I said, quietly this time. Stella remained silent.

I heard Tristan's chewing and a child running through the apartment above us. Outside on the street somebody was whistling a light and cheerful tune.

After a minute or two, Stella rose slowly from her chair. I grabbed her hand to hold her back, but she pulled it away and left. I ran after her. Tristan stayed seated and called out, "I don't want to think about what will happen to you if you tell anyone—and I mean anyone—about the delicacies you saw here."

I followed her out, but at the entryway she came to a stop.

"Leave me, I need to be alone now."

"Can't I help somehow?"

"Please, let me go."

I let Stella go, watched the door close behind her, and lingered awhile in the hall, just standing there. What kind of man was I, not to have followed her? I think I knew I was incapable of helping her in this moment. But for the first time, I understood the value of playing a part. I told myself there was nothing I wouldn't do for her, given the chance. Turning around, I walked calmly back into the apartment. Tristan chewed and smiled up at me.

"Thanks for still being here," he said.

I hated myself. I wanted to shout at him, but that wouldn't have helped Stella.

I took a couple of breaths. "What can we do?" I asked.

"Be strong and forget her."

"You call that being strong?"

Tristan shrugged his shoulders. He began piling a plate with cheese and eggs and spreading butter thickly on a slice of rye bread. He stood up, walked around the table, and put the plate in front of me; with the other hand he touched my shoulder.

"Please. I so dislike eating alone."

I ate a couple of bites but tasted nothing

"You should eat more bread," said Tristan. "Sourdough. Bread is good for you."

I pushed my plate away.

Tristan shook his head gently, took a piece of rolled-up cheese, and tossed it in front of Muck's muzzle. The cheese stayed there, untouched.

"I want you to help her."

Tristan sighed and threw up his hands. "I've been helping her for a long time," he said softly.

I leaned forward, waiting.

"This forger that she's supposed to find . . ." Tristan said.

"How do you know about that?"

His eyes were bright. I realized then that he was on the inside, that he knew much more than I did.

"If she catches him, she can save her parents. I mean, a girl like that, with her contacts. For the comrades on Burgstrasse she's the perfect decoy Jew."

I didn't know what to think anymore.

"'Decoy Jew,'" Tristan said to himself. "Outstanding phrase."

I felt rage rising in me again. "You really scared her."

"Scared her? She's scared me. She's dragging both of us down with her, so quickly that you can't even see it."

Tristan looked straight at me.

"Do you think it's easy for me? I'm completely worn out. That's how it is with a dancing bear like that. You get your paws singed, even when you treat it kindly."

Not wanting to anger Tristan, I slowly emptied my plate and drank beer with him.

"Yes, that's how it is with dancing bears," he said, and then, "Can we talk about something else?"

He talked about how afraid he was of Muck's death and how hard it was to find a suitable woman when you were as tall as he was. He changed the subject as if Stella's life were a minor concern. He said he wanted to have a family and children and that he would like to have a daughter the most, because of all the pretty dresses he could buy her. I kept silent. Later we listened to one of his new swing records, and he danced a little.

"If it weren't so peculiar, I would ask you to join me," he said.

"Do you really believe that?" I asked.

"What?"

"What you said. That the Jews want to hack us to pieces?"

Tristan swayed to the music. "Of course not."

He moved his hand to the beat as he continued.

"The Israelites are different from us. I believe that. The whole propaganda thing is important because it allows the rabble to grasp that. They can do a lot of good things, too, the Israelites; with money, for example, and they make fabulous fur coats. I gladly listen to Jew music sometimes. The clarinet glissando at the beginning of 'Rhapsody in Blue.' Outstanding. And, just between us, I find Sephardic Israelite girls quite appealing. But the Israelite in itself is another thing entirely. They smell different, too."

"That's absurd. They don't smell different."

"They do, admit it. You should know best; they smell different, Jewish. Like little Kristin." He smiled. "Some men like it."

Then his face grew serious.

"Do you think little Kristin will keep quiet? I mean, if my employer finds out that I had cheese sent from Paris . . ."

I shook my head. "She's not like that."

Tristan nodded. He bent near me. "The squirrel is doing very well."

"What?"

"Once it was back on its feet, it returned to the chestnut branch."

"But you said Mademoiselle Lechaux got rid of it."

"A white lie, Fritz." He winked. "See? Just a white lie."

He looked at me.

"Fritz?"

"Yes."

"Why are you still here?"

"I didn't want to leave you to eat alone."

"This is no place for someone like you."

"What do you mean?"

"Berlin. This crazy city. This Germany. You are made of finer cloth."

When I returned to my room in the Grand Hotel, Stella was lying awake in the dark. Before I could tell her about my conversation with Tristan, she said, "Tomorrow I will find Cioma Schönhaus."

Her voice sounded the way it had earlier in the year; her strength had returned. For a moment my breath caught.

"You can't do that."

"I have to."

"You mustn't."

I watched as she rolled over on the mattress, turning her back to me.

"I know," she said.

*

Cases #36 and #37:   2 Unknown Persons
Witness: Hedwig H.

The witness and her husband observed the accused lead two men out of the Café Kranzler on the Kurfürstendamm and speak with them in a friendly manner. The Jewish informer G. was there, along with SS-Führer S., in civilian dress. After S. showed his badge, he ordered both persons to climb into his car. The accused then left.

P. II / 20

June 1942

More than one thousand bombers in the Royal Air Force bombard Bremen for seventy-five minutes. The last Jewish schools in the German Reich are closed. Paul McCartney is born. With few exceptions, half-Jews are no longer permitted to study at university. The sixth of Dr. Joseph Goebbels's Ten Commandments for Every National Socialist is issued: "He who defames Germany defames you and your dead; punch back." The U.S. Congress approves $42 billion for armaments. The Reich Health Office extolls a drink called "Biomalz," made by the Patermann company, as important for the "Development of strong youth for the march into the future." Hot plates found in the possession of Jewish Germans are to be confiscated. In Berlin shop windows hang signs that say: "Attention! Spies! Mind your words!" In Munich, Hans Scholl and Alexander Schmorell found a resistance group and call it "the White Rose." Reinhard Heydrich dies of peritonitis, likely caused by a piece of his car seat that had penetrated his abdominal cavity after the explosion. As retaliation for the attempt on his life, German policemen kill the male residents of the village of Lidice, deport the women and children to a concentration camp, and bulldoze the place. The assassins had no connection to Lidice.

*

Only a couple of weeks before, we had listened to music together and laughed about Schwanenwerder. Now all was quiet.

She was protecting her family. Could that be wrong?

I was a young man with money and a Swiss passport who had thought he could live in the middle of this war without having anything to do with it. I had come as a tourist. I had been stupid. I kept silent because everything I thought of saying sounded wrong. I didn't tell Stella about Tristan because I didn't understand what he was up to. Not fully.

She lay in bed with her back to me. Her skin was hot, as if she had a fever. Stella took my arm and pressed it against her stomach.

"I can't be intimate tonight."

I kissed her neck.

"Will you hold me?" she asked.

We lay awake like that for a long time. I thought of home and of the sunflower field of my childhood, or maybe I dreamed it, it made no difference.

Later Stella trembled in my arms. The curtains in our bedroom stayed open. The sun lit up the room in the early morning.

"Are you asleep?" Stella whispered.

"Yes," I said.

I filled the bathtub with warm water for her, and when she sat in the water, I washed her underarms and her back and washed her carefully between her legs. She looked at me while I went about it. I helped her get dressed. She took one of the chocolates from her handbag and ate it. I helped her get into her suit. She put on her little Tyrolean hunting hat.

"Where are we going?" I asked.

"You don't need to know," she said.

I kissed her eyelids. "I'm your man now."

I felt my heart leap as I said that. I didn't know if I was saying it for her or for me. For the first time since she had been in Burgstrasse, I saw her smile.

"My man," she said, and leaned her forehead against my chin.

"What do we do now?" I asked.

Stella took a step away and looked at me from a short distance. I didn't know how she saw it, but I knew what we were doing.

We called for a taxi. As we got in, Stella said, "To the hospital in Iranische Street, please," then we drove through Berlin and looked at the people who were going to work, shopping, sitting on benches and reading newspapers. People were doing the things people do on a Wednesday morning. Everything looked normal.

I asked myself what would happen to the forger if he were taken to Burgstrasse. I leaned in close to Stella's ear. "Is there no other way?"

She looked out the window.

The hospital looked big and labyrinthine. Since Stella had come into my life, she had decided where we went, what we ate, where we lived. I'd liked it. She was a strong woman; I was weak. But that day I couldn't take it anymore.

Before she walked into the hospital, I grabbed her hand. "What are we doing here?"

A man was walking out the door. Stella and I kept silent. She pulled me into the courtyard. She spoke quickly.

"As a Jew in Berlin, you can only escape if you have cash or a false identity card."

A man with a bouquet in his hand walked past.

"Put your arms around me," Stella said.

I embraced her. She whispered in my ear.

"Here at the hospital there's an internist who's a quarter Jewish. He's allowed to continue working. Every Jew in Berlin knows that for six hundred Reichsmarks he will make you a Sicherheitsdienst identity pass."

"Schönhaus?"

"He will lead us to him."

We held each other.

"It's nice, the way you hold me tight," she said.

I felt sick. I told myself it was because I hadn't had breakfast, but I knew that wasn't true.

"I can't do it."

"A person can do a lot when he wants to."

"I can't pull it off."

She laid her cheek against mine. "Then wait in the hotel."

"Stella . . ."

"It's Kristin. Call me Kristin."

Her lips were cold. I didn't move as she straightened her shoulders and twisted her mouth into a smile. I saw how hard this was for her. With head held high she went off to the hospital entrance and disappeared inside.

I walked aimlessly through the streets. It was a humid morning; the asphalt steamed. The paths were sticky with resin from the pollen of the lindens.

I threw up in a cobblestone driveway and spat out white foam. A handsome young man in a Hitler Youth uniform was walking behind me on the sidewalk. When he saw me leaning against the wall for support, he hurried up to me, put a hand on my shoulder, and asked if he could help me.

Sunk in thought I walked through Berlin until I came to the Spree. I asked a woman who was gathering wood to point out the way to the Reichstag and went to the Grand Hotel. At some stage I reached into the pocket of my jacket and felt paper between my fingers. It was one of Stella's handwritten notes: "Thank you for being my home."

Dusk was falling when I got to the hotel. In the elevator I met the one-armed man.

"Heil Hitler, sir," he said.

"Good evening. May I ask you something?"

"Of course, sir."

"How did you lose your arm?"

The man straightened up; his neck got longer. "Grenade attack, Poland, Paratrooper Regiment Two, sir. We overran the Polacks, and a grenade got through."

I stayed silent.

Before I got out of the elevator, he said, "One more thing, if you permit, sir."

"Yes."

"'Lose' is the wrong word. The arm was taken from me."

Stella came in the morning. I noticed her only when she pulled my arm across her as she lay beside me.

"So?" I asked.

Only one word, but death was hidden within it.

"I have to do this alone, dear Fritz. Please don't ask me anything else."

Whenever she thought she might hurt me, she called me "dear Fritz." I laid my face on her body. She stroked my cheek. I didn't want to lie, so I stayed silent a long time.

"Stella?" I asked at some point.

"Mm-hmm."

"Your name?"

"What about it?"

"Are you named for the North Star?"

She hesitated as she thought about it. "No," she said. I fell asleep on her back.

As the sun was going down, she woke me, grabbing me. I was inside her before I was completely awake. She breathed loudly through her mouth. After a couple of minutes she started to sob.

"Don't leave me," she cried in my ear.

I shook my head and kissed her tears. "I promise."

"Don't leave me."

I looked into her eyes. "I will never leave you," I said, "I promise."

When the sun had set, Stella went to the bath to wash. I wanted to help her, but she said she would do it alone.

In the bedroom I took off the sheets. In my head I was assembling the first steps of a plan. Her blood had dripped onto the mattress.

*

Case #1: Edith Z.
          Witness: Erna E.

The witness Erna E. was meeting up with her niece Edith Z., both of them illegal residents, at the subway station at Uhlandstrasse. The accused suddenly appeared and ordered Edith Z. to follow her, with the words, "Come quickly, you must go to the camp, otherwise I'll get the

Gestapo." Not until Edith Z. called out, "It's Stella," as she was departing did witness E. understand what was happening. She states that Edith Z. was transported to the Grosse Hamburger Strasse camp and later was killed at Auschwitz.

Pp. I / 44R
Pp. I / 185

July 1942

Germans kill around ten thousand inhabitants of the ghetto of Slonim in Belorussia. By order of the Reich education minister, half-Jews are no longer permitted to attend elementary schools, middle schools, or high schools; the exception for quarter-Jews remains in effect. In Munich the Sixth Great German Art Exhibition opens with works by 680 artists. FC Schalke 04 wins 2–0 against Vienna-Wien and becomes the German soccer champion for the sixth time. S. Fischer Verlag announces it will publish the collected works of Gerhart Hauptmann on the occasion of Hauptmann's eightieth birthday. Forty-four Lancaster bombers of the Royal Air Force bombard Danzig; ninety people die. The seventh commandment of Dr. Joseph Goebbels's Ten Commandments for Every National Socialist is issued: "If a ruffian gives you trouble, give him more trouble in return. If someone denies you your rights, remember that only your own action can preserve them." Adolf Hitler relocates his headquarters from East Prussia to Ukraine for a few months; the new quarters, built shortly before, are given the name "Werewolf." Heinrich Himmler, Reichsführer, informs his colleagues that the people and animals residing at the Auschwitz camp are at their disposal for medical experiments. As part of his research, Professor Hans Holfelder will explore the possibility of sterilizing the inferior races and the mentally ill through radiation.

*

We drank too much, too early. We danced joylessly in the yellow salon. I thought about Stella's parents. She ironed my shirts, devoting special attention to the shoulder seams.

I gave her Father's metal box with the rose pattern. Beforehand I ran my finger around the edge counterclockwise three times.

We walked at sunset along the banks of the Spree. We talked less than before; my laughter was only half true. She ate more of her Pervitin chocolates.

At a pharmacy I inquired about Pervitin. It cost two Reichsmarks for a box with ten chocolates. The pharmacist was a young woman who wore round glasses and had her hair tied in a ponytail.

"May I ask you about these?" I asked, pointing to the boxes on the shelf.

"That's what I'm here for."

"What is it they do?"

"They suppress fatigue, hunger, and pain. And they give a person the feeling that he's strong as an ox."

"And are they dangerous?"

"How do you define dangerous?"

"Are they addictive?"

"Yes."

"Do they change you?"

"The Wehrmacht has already ordered a million doses from Temmler, so they can't be all that bad. How many do you want?"

I bought five packages and tied a ribbon around them that I bought in a flower shop. When I gave them to Stella, she stroked my face with the palm of her hand from my forehead, down over my closed eyelids, to my chin.

In those days, Stella often said she needed time to herself. "To find myself," she called it. She disappeared into the city in the morning and came back to the hotel in the evening.

"What did you do?" I asked.

"Nothing special.

"Do you trust me?" she asked.

I didn't, but I nodded.

She went alone to the theater and to the Deutsche Oper and saw *The Magic Flute*. I gave her the money. She hummed the bird catcher's melody. Once she said that she thought it was beautiful, the way Papageno and Papagena had found each other, two monsters who recognized one another.

I tried to convince myself that it was fine that she had the freedom to do as she liked. Sometimes I took the circle line around Berlin for hours just to make the time pass. I sat by the window at night, looked out on the street, and thought about Cioma Schönhaus. She'd said she had to do it alone, but it wasn't true.

*

Cases #28 and #29:   *Abraham and Moritz Z.*
                                 Witnesses: 1. Abraham Z., 2.
                                 Moritz Z.

The married couple Z., illegal residents, were with their son and daughter at the Unter den Linden opera and sat apart during the production. After the performance, the accused grabbed their son, Moritz, by the belt of his coat with the words, "You are Mr. Z." He broke free, slapped the accused in the face, and ran away. The accused called out, "Arrest him! Jew!" Passersby followed him and pulled him by the hair back to the opera house, where the accused stood with Rolf I. and a police official. The father, Abraham Z., who had already fled the opera with his wife, seeing the crowd of people, came back and punched Rolf I. in the face with the words, "We are not criminals, we are Jews." Abraham and Moritz Z. were taken to the camp on Grosse Hamburger Strasse. During the course of interrogation by the camp director Dobberke, who inquired about the whereabouts of Mrs. Z., the accused was present. She said to Abraham Z., "I saw your wife too, she must be here." Abraham and Moritz Z. succeeded in escaping after two weeks.

Pp. I / 107, 193–194
Pp. I / 17, 42, 191–192

*

At the bar, one of the guests said the Royal Air Force would leave Berlin in ashes. The luggage of hotel guests who wanted to leave the country stood in the lobby and the hallways.

One hot and sticky July night we couldn't sleep.

"Let's go outside for a little while," said Stella.

We put on our coats and left the hotel. We heard singing coming from a pub on Torstrasse. A group of soldiers in dark uniforms was settled in there, drinking. Stella held my hand.

"Let's go in there," she said.

I didn't move.

"I want to sing," she said.

Inside, the windowpanes were damp from body heat. It was dark throughout the city; electricity had been cut off. Oil lamps lit the bar, and there were cardboard screens in front of the windows so no light could leak out. A couple of soldiers had taken off their jackets and were leaning against the bar in their undershirts. They looked like they'd all gone together to the barbershop earlier in the evening and asked for the same haircut.

Each one had his blood type tattooed on the inside left upper arm. There were a lot of young women in the pub, drinking sweet vermouth from water glasses. Girls with braided pigtails served behind the bar.

Stella asked one of the girls who the men were, and she said with shining cheeks that it was the SS Viking Panzer Division. Early tomorrow they were heading to the front.

The air smelled of sour sweat and of the girls' wartime perfume, fake jasmine.

Stella went to the bar and ordered two Berliner Kindl beers. We stood crowded together and drank in silence. The beer tasted of dishwashing liquid. It was wartime beer with a low alcohol content.

"Come on, let's not be so boring," Stella said. From time to time one of the men would start singing a song. I'd almost gotten used to the sight of soldiers, but these were different: they drank more, they talked louder, and they were all bigger than me. Their uniforms were dark. Stella sang along to the songs. It was loud in the bar.

"Shoot up the Slavs and the Hebrews will fall," said a soldier with a deep, rich voice. He looked good and gentle, like the herdsmen on Mont Blanc. There were a few Greek letters tattooed under his right collarbone. My ancient Greek was bad, but I could read it because I knew the story. It said: "*Molon labe.*"

Stella laughed and raised her glass as the word "Hebrews" rang out. One of the men shouted, "*Sieg!*" and stretched his arm high. Stella also called out, "*Sieg!*"

The tattooed soldier ordered two glasses of corn liquor at the bar and clinked glasses with Stella. He said something in her ear that I couldn't make out, and she laughed. He ordered more corn liquor and didn't give me a glass.

Stella turned her back to me; the tattooed man looked at me over her shoulder.

Next to me stood a slim man whom I'd overlooked at first. In his hand he held a glass of carbonated mineral water. He was twenty years old at most, wore no uniform, just a rough linen shirt, and he had a precisely combed side part, which he'd fixed with pomade. He jabbed his elbow in my ribs and bent close to me. "Your girl?"

I nodded.

"The guy?"

"I . . . he's a soldier," I said.

The young man next to me smiled. "May I take care of it?"

The man was small and pale. He raised his left hand with the water glass as high as his cheekbone.

"Berlin champion welterweight."

The tattooed man got closer to Stella.

"You're a boxer?" I asked.

"Former. No official bouts anymore."

"Why not?"

"I'm not allowed."

I saw the pain in his face.

"I'm Fritz," I said, and took his hand.

"Isaac," he said.

I saw that the tattooed man had his hand on Stella's lower back. I was shocked. I felt hot; my stomach flipped.

"Don't say that name out loud."

"Why not?"

The bar had a wooden floor; there was mold in the corners.

"I could be one of them," I said.

134

"But you're not."

For a moment his lips touched my earlobe, he came so close: "Do you want to see an Untermensch land a punch?"

He gave me his glass of mineral water.

He took the time to fold his shirtsleeves up over his elbows. With care he laid cloth over cloth. I saw dark, swollen veins through the skin on the underside of his arm. He unbuckled his belt and rebuckled it one notch tighter, then he cracked his neck, to the right, to the left. He adjusted his stance, thrust his left foot forward, and put his weight on the balls of his feet. This was how he approached the tattooed man. He stuck his thumbs in the waistband of his pants.

He didn't say a word. As soon as he came near enough to touch the man, who now had both his hands on Stella's backside, he paused, raised his open hands up by his head as if to smooth his hair, shifted his weight to the back, and without warning flung his right fist past Stella's head and into the face of the tattooed man. It sounded as if someone had dropped a heavy stone into wet grass.

The soldier let go of Stella, fell back, and hit his head on the floor. He stayed lying there.

Immediately, half a dozen soldiers turned toward Isaac, who was already on the way to the door. He didn't run; he moved quickly but without haste. An infantryman stood in his way. Isaac went up to him, and when the man threw a punch at him, he made a barely visible movement with his upper body so the fist grazed his hair. He kept going.

As Isaac reached the door to the street, he turned around and looked my way. Just for an instant, we looked each other in the eye. I would always remember it. I still think about it today sometimes, when I need strength. I think about Isaac and his gray eyes. The perfect part in his hair.

When one of the soldiers jumped him, Isaac punched him to the floor with a seamless left hook. The soldier slumped to his knees in front of him and stayed that way.

Soldiers ran after Isaac. But I knew he would be fine.

Stella grabbed my hand. "Who was that?"

"Why did you let him touch you that way?"

"Did you send him to get rid of the guy for me?"

"You are my woman, Stella, nobody but me is allowed to touch you."

She put both her hands around my neck. She was drunk.

"Why did you do that?" I asked.

"What? Can't I enjoy life a little? Who was that?"

"That was Isaac."

I led Stella by the hand out of the bar. I felt like a conqueror even though I hadn't won anything.

As we walked home across the cobblestones of Torstrasse, Stella said without looking at me, "Isaac?"

"Yes."

"A Jew?" she asked.

"A friend," I said.

*

Case #35:   S.

Witness: Fanny S.

*In the year 1942 the witness Fanny S. found herself
in the documentation bureau for Jews in Pfalzburger
Street· The accused, who was present, took her personal household file from her hands and ordered her
to wait while she locked the door. Upon request, the
accused showed the witness an identity card on which
was written: "This woman is authorized to take ac-
tive measures in Jewish affairs. Public agencies are
requested to assist her!" The back of the pass featured
a passport photo and an official stamp. Through the
intervention of the director of the documents bureau,
the witness was allowed to go, as she was "Aryan."
Three or four other Jewish women who had been previ-
ously detained in the documents bureau were taken
away.*

Pp. II / 44, 186a

*

Stella slapped me in the face when I told her my plan. She
hit harder than I would have expected.

"Don't make fun of me," she said.

I waited with my head sunk low for the next slap.

"For God's sake," she said, and paced up and down the
room.

After a while she stopped and laid her hand on my cheek. I started when she touched me.

"It's really red," she said.

"It's all right."

"Did I hurt you?"

I kissed her forehead.

"Maybe we should try it," she said. "But Dobberke, the director of the Grosse Hamburger Strasse camp, you're no match for him, Fritz."

I had written to Father about Stella after getting his letter from Istanbul, and I had written to him again after her return from Burgstrasse. Father spoke with an industrialist friend from Franconia. An express courier brought an envelope with a letter that said Toni and Gerhard Goldschlag were needed in a weaving mill in Weissenburg because of their expertise in tailoring. The writing was formulated to make it sound like the Goldschlags' work in Weissenburg was directly connected to the Final Victory. In the envelope there was also a short letter with a swastika in the letterhead, signed by the gauleiter of Middle Franconia.

I was freezing and sweating as I rode in the taxi to Grosse Hamburger Strasse. I stroked the scar on my cheek. I felt the wind from the open window blow through my hair.

Grosse Hamburger Strasse was more like a lane, so narrow that you could drive down only one side of it.

Stella had told me that the camp was near a cobbler's shop, in a pale, massive building that formerly had been the Jewish old folks' home. In the basement there were dungeons that were so cold that many nights the prisoners, chained together, walked in circles until dawn so they wouldn't freeze to death.

There was a furniture truck parked near the entrance that said "Feinstein and Sons" on it.

A watchman asked for my papers and saluted when I handed him my Swiss passport. That happened more and more often. Many Germans weren't sure how they were supposed to classify me, and since it could cost you your life to annoy the wrong man these days, even policemen often acted deferentially out of caution. The watchman led me down a long corridor to Dobberke.

He sat at a desk in his office, a remarkably muscular man who had shaved both sides of his head and parted his hair at the top of his skull. His dimples suggested that he liked to laugh; the circles under his eyes and the thinness of his skin suggested that he drank a lot and slept little. The pores on his cheeks reminded me of Mother.

Dobberke's shirt was too tight in the collar. His right ear was bigger than his left. His irises were of a paleness I had rarely seen.

Two glasses and a milk bottle filled with a clear liquid were set out on the table in front of Dobberke. Across from him sat a young woman in a nurse's uniform, with a starched cap on her head. She smiled when I walked in. The room smelled of gun oil and smoked pork. I held my hands crossed behind my back so nobody could see how much they were shaking.

139

"Ah, wonderful, just what the doctor ordered," said Dobberke.

He took a pack of cards out of the breast pocket of his drill jacket and slapped it on the table. A little owl was printed on the backs of the cards.

"We need a third."

I stood as straight as I could. "I've come to speak to you about the Goldschlag prisoners. I have a letter here . . ."

"Hold your horses, comrade. Let's have a tipple for starters, then a little round of cards." Dobberke was slurring his speech a little. He nodded at the nurse. "Glass," he said.

She rose, went to a cupboard, and took out a glass. On the shelf above the glass was a bullwhip, aligned with the edge of the cupboard door.

As the woman set the glass on the table, Dobberke grabbed the backs of her knees from behind and let his hands linger there for a while.

"Elli here mixes the best home brew in all Berlin. Tell him your secret."

The woman kept smiling; she ignored his hands. "I take the hundred percent alcohol from the surgery and then add a lot of sugar," she said, giggling.

I sat down. Dobberke pulled a piece of salt pork wrapped in cloth from his jacket pocket and cut thick slices.

"Prewar quality," he said.

"Nice," I said.

Dobberke dealt me cards. "We're playing skat, no low trumps. Split, three rounds of Bock, three of Ramsch. Virgin doubles points for the loser. *Capito?*"

I had never played skat. "In Switzerland we play jass," I said.

Dobberke said nothing. He closed his eyes for a bit as if he were listening to a soft voice that was speaking to him. The nurse shifted on her chair. She looked at me. Maybe her glance was a warning; it also could have been scorn. Dobberke opened his eyes.

"*Ca-pi-to?*" he asked again, pronouncing each syllable separately.

I shuffled the deck

Once, while staying overnight at an inn in Vorarlberg after a trip to Vienna, I had played a game called steigerer. At the time, someone had told me it was a lot like this German card game skat. I kept on shuffling. I didn't know how I was supposed to deal out the cards.

"Someone died once from overshuffling. I think it was in Övelgönne," said Dobberke. Then he pounded the table with the flat of his hand and laughed. The nurse didn't laugh. That didn't seem to bother Dobberke.

I gave each person three cards. Dobberke took them and whistled through his teeth. I saw the nurse tap briefly on the table once with two fingers. I laid two cards on the table. Then I dealt out the rest.

Dobberke kept whistling. "Eighteen," he said. "Eight! Ten!" With him every syllable seemed to come with an exclamation point.

"Pass," said the nurse.

Both of them looked at me. The nurse nodded barely perceptibly to the right.

"Pass," I said.

Dobberke smiled, his mouth stretched wide. "Grand hand!" he shouted. Then he poked the nurse's right breast with his left forefinger, leaned his head forward, and said, "With the grand you play aces, otherwise shut your faces."

"Yes, sir, Herr Hauptscharführer," said the nurse. Then she played the queen of hearts. I played a heart. Dobberke won again. From the corner of my eye I saw the nurse drink great gulps of her home brew. The liquid tasted as sweet as quince syrup and burned the throat.

"To the German U-boat fleet," said Dobberke, and raised his glass.

We stood up to toast, sat back down, and kept playing. It was a quiet game. For a long time the only sounds in the room were the turning over of cards, the rumbling of Dobberke's stomach, and the banging of glasses on the wooden tabletop. When Dobberke drew his knife through the salt pork it made no sound. He licked the blade.

Someone knocked. The watchman opened the door.

"Kaltwitz is here."

Dobberke smiled and sucked air between his teeth. "Hurly-burly," he said, emptied his glass, and left the room with the watchman.

The nurse and I looked at each other across the tabletop.

"What does 'hurly-burly' mean?" I asked.

She breathed steadily. "What does it mean . . . ? It means that now a man's going to get his teeth kicked in. Usually it just takes one kick."

I couldn't read her face. "Are you a couple?" I asked.

She took a breath and smiled her flawless smile. I thought I could smell the powder on her skin. She drank a sip. She didn't respond. I looked at her while I thought about it. As I was reflecting, she said, "You are a terrible actor. Eat some of that bacon or you'll be soused on top of it."

"What do you mean, 'actor'?"

"'What do I mean, actor.' Your lips were quivering the whole time."

I bit my lip. She pushed the cutting board over to me. I pushed it back.

"Thanks for the help with the cards."

"I didn't help anybody." Looking at the board, she said, "And I don't eat pork."

Dobberke came back; he carried a drill jacket over one arm and had rolled up his shirtsleeves high. Drops of sweat beaded his temples. A blood vessel pulsed at his throat. His right hand was in a leather glove.

"In some ways I like the Jews, too," he said. He kissed the nurse on the neck and nodded to me. He drank and raised his glass in a toast: "To the destruction of Judah."

"Prost."

He looked at me. "What is this asshole actually doing here?"

I took the letter out of the pocket of my coat, which was draped over the back of the chair. "I'm just the messenger," I said, and gave the letter to Dobberke. He read.

That's how it feels. To lie.

"Forget about it, comrade," said Dobberke, before he'd read to the end.

"Just a minute," I said, "my client asked me to tell you that he would be happy to recognize your service to the Fatherland with payment in kind."

"Quit talking like such an egghead asshole. What do you mean?"

"As compensation for the inconvenience, my client would like to recognize your work with five liters of rum and six pounds of bacon. Franconian bacon. Pork belly."

I was sweating so much that you could see the sweat stains on my suit jacket.

"What's the stuff called?" asked Dobberke.

"Wammerl, cold smoked pork belly."

I don't know how I came up with that idea in the moment. The bacon thing I had planned ahead of time, but I don't know how I hit upon Franconian bacon.

"Wammerl." Dobberke considered for a moment. "To the German U-boat fleet. Prost," he said, and after a pause, "Do you know about *salo*?"

"No."

"That's what they call their bacon in the east. Damned good stuff. I ate it while I was visiting the German armaments factory in Lemberg. White, very fine. They let it cure for a month in wooden chests in the cellar. It melts on the tongue. *Salo*."

Dobberke licked his lips.

"*Salo*," said the nurse.

"I'll make sure you get the best bacon possible," I said.

"Oh, shut your face," he said. "Ten."

"Excuse me?"

"Ten pounds."

"Nine," I said, so as not to cause suspicion.

"Ten, stop bartering, you Jew."

He inspected me. Sweat rolled down my face. Dobberke came closer.

"Why are you sweating so much, comrade?"

I could tell that my lips were quivering, though I was keeping my teeth clamped together. "I'm not."

"Something's off here," he said, "I thought so earlier."

"The rum . . ." I wiped the sweat off my forehead.

"I knew the whole time that something was off, Elli," he said. He grabbed her neck with one hand. "This damned heating, did you turn it up again?"

"Sorry, my Hauptscharführer," said the nurse.

He turned to me without letting go of her. "Ten."

I wanted to shake Dobberke's hand. "Ten, agreed," I said.

"I shit on your sweaty handshake. And now, clear out."

I nodded to him, made a quick bow to the nurse, and looked her in the face for a moment before I left the room.

I walked all the way down the long, linoleum-floored corridor to the exit and felt my knees trembling with every step. I didn't hear the steps behind me. When a hand touched my shoulder, I was terrified. The nurse was standing so near that the tips of our toes touched when I turned around.

"Come with me," she said.

I shook my head.

"Come with me, I'll take you to the inmates." A muscle in her face twitched.

"To the Goldschlags?"

"Two minutes, no longer."

We climbed up a staircase. In the corridor hung old, cheap paintings, German landscapes that must have been hanging here when the house was still an old folks home. The higher we climbed, the more piercing the stink of sweat, urine, and destroyed lives became. The silence stunned me. We heard only our steps on the rubber floor. I stopped, grabbed the woman's elbow, and said so only she could hear:

"The furniture truck outside . . ."

"Shh . . ." she said.

"But the furniture trucks, the rumor."

The woman pushed a strand of sweat-dampened hair off my forehead before looking me in the eyes. She said, "In this country, only the pretty stories are rumors. The ugly ones are all true."

She hugged me. She pushed her arms through mine, under my shoulders, around my back, and held me close. "Run away, you idiot," she said softly in my ear. She let go of me as suddenly as she had first touched me and went away without looking at me.

The nurse spoke with a watchman. The man looked at a list, took a big bunch of keys from the wall, and we followed him to one of the doors in the corridor, which were all locked on the outside with an iron bar.

The room was perhaps twenty square meters in size; inside there were so many people that there was hardly enough space for them to lie down. They watched us. The window was half walled up, the glass in it fitted with bars. In some places there was straw on the floor. A wave of stale, warm air from the room washed over us.

"Goldschlag!" the watchman bellowed into the room. In his hand he carried a wooden stick that looked like a sawed-off broom handle.

147

When the watchman shouted, the people in the room flinched. I heard faint words but couldn't understand them. Two small, stooped forms moved toward the door, climbing over others along the way. They held each other's hands.

Stella's mother had the same fair hair as her daughter. The Goldschlags were wearing winter coats and looked down at the floor in front of the watchman. Stella's father held a filthy bundle in his hand; I didn't know what was in it.

"We are Toni and Gerhard Goldschlag," he said, his head bent low between his shoulders.

"Step forward," said the watchman, sounding bored, rather than hostile.

The Goldschlags stepped into the hall. As I reached my hand out to Stella's mother she drew back as though I had been going to hit her.

"I know your daughter," I said.

Frau Goldschlag raised her eyes; her husband continued looking at the floor. "They want . . ." he said.

His left pant leg turned dark.

She was so thin that you could see the veins in her neck; her head shook slightly, as if she had a tremor. The collar of her blouse had been white once.

"Stella," she said, almost expressionlessly.

"She is doing well."

The watchman stood alongside, listening. He rapped the forged bar on the door rhythmically with his wooden stick. Frau Goldschlag spoke quickly and softly.

"Please, could you please tell Stella that we're also doing well?"

"I will."

"Tell her that we are warm here. Clean. Bedding of home-spun linen."

Her words came thick and fast.

"Tell her that they've got coil spring mattresses here, and every day we have porridge with a dab of butter, and sometimes we even listen to the radio."

The watchman laughed. He was missing an eyetooth. *Tock tock tock* went the stick.

"They want us . . ." said Herr Goldschlag.

In the cell I heard someone groan.

Stella's mother gripped the sleeve of my jacket.

"Hands off, Jew," said the watchman, his tone still peaceful. His stick kept rapping. I looked at the drops on the linoleum.

"Tell her that I'm getting watercolor paints, and that Papa plays Schumann on the piano every day and has the same sense of humor as the camp director. And that we will soon be free again."

"But that's a lie."

"Stella must stop," said the mother.

"Stella . . . Stop what?"

The watchman's stick pounded.

Tears rolled down Frau Goldschlag's cheeks and left behind light tracks. "He doesn't know," she said to herself.

Tock tock tock.

"Our future," said Herr Goldschlag.

"Be quiet, Gerhard."

"They want to take our future away."

"He doesn't know," said Frau Goldschlag.

"What don't I know?"

She didn't have to say it. I had known the whole time. The watchman smiled; he didn't stop drumming, *tock tock.*

I grabbed the stick with my hand and held it still. Just for a second.

The next day I bought five bottles of rum and ten pounds of bacon, not from Franconia but from the Grand Hotel's head chef. The price was high.

Toni and Gerhard Goldschlag remained imprisoned in the Grosse Hamburger Strasse camp. Dobberke broke his word, just like that, because he could.

At night Stella talked in her sleep, and I held her stomach the way she liked. Long after midnight she said something that sounded like "Neschume," but maybe I misheard, or maybe I dreamed it.

*

Case #22:   Kurt C.
         Witness: Kurt C.

The witness Kurt C. was crossing Rosenthaler Platz when he suddenly saw the accused coming toward him.

Because she was already known to him as a catcher, he ran away. While Rolf I. pursued him, along with a number of other citizens, the accused entered a telephone booth. C. was caught by his pursuers and brought back to Rosenthaler Platz, where Gestapo officials arrested him and delivered him to the Grosse Hamburger Strasse camp. He succeeded in escaping four months later.

Pp. I / 15, 112, 188

August 1942

To ensure a steady food supply, the transfer or change of owner-
ship of German agricultural properties is forbidden. Members
of the Sonderkommando lead the Carmelite nun Edith Stein
into a sealed room in Auschwitz and fill the room with Zyklon
B gas. In India the police arrest the activist Mohandas K. Gandhi. The commander of the Sixth Army gives the order to attack
Stalingrad. In the USA, the film *Bambi* celebrates its premiere.
Near Stalingrad an Italian cavalry division attacks Soviet soldiers;
many of the riders and horses die. This is the last use of cavalry
in this war. The industrial manufacture of penicillin begins. The
Gestapo imprison members of the Berlin resistance group the
Red Orchestra; many of the prisoners will be put to death at Plöt-
zensee. The eighth commandment of Dr. Joseph Goebbels's Ten
Commandments for Every National Socialist is issued: "Don't be
a rowdy anti-Semite, but beware of the *Berliner Tageblatt*." The
head of the German civil government in Serbia, Harald Turner,
reports: "Serbia is the only land in which the Jewish Question
and the Gypsy question have been solved." Janusz Korczak, the
head of the orphanage in the Warsaw ghetto, goes of his own
free will with two hundred children to the death camp of Treb-
linka and allows himself to be killed; Korczak holds two of the
youngest children in his arms. Heinrich Himmler proclaims
"Luftwaffe Gray" the new color for German fire engines.

*

Father insisted on meeting Stella. He took a car to Vienna and, from there, the train, because on his last flight, he'd gotten caught in a blizzard, and the plane had been forced to make an emergency landing with an iced-up cockpit.

The locomotive belched clouds of smoke into the train concourse. We drove to the hotel and sat in Father's room in two armchairs and drank arak with ice water.

Father told me that he had learned on his journey that American troops soon would be coming to Germany. I got up and knelt beside my father's armchair.

"I'm afraid, Papa."

"Do you love her?"

"I think so."

"Then I'm afraid, too."

Stella was filling the bath with water when I walked into our room. She was reading a book by Vicki Baum, sitting on the edge of the tub and drinking chilled champagne.

"Papa likes you."

She kissed me for a long time. "I was so afraid I would do something wrong," she said.

"No need for that."

"I can't speak as elegantly as you do."

I saw one of her notes on the narrow granite shelf under the bathroom mirror: "Do you still love me?"

That night we wanted to go to the hotel restaurant. The

food was still good, despite the rationing. In the wine cellar there were still a few barrels of Châteauneuf-du-Pape.

Father and I waited at the bar. Stella had forgotten the time. When I left the room in my dinner jacket, she was sitting naked in front of her vanity table. I've never understood men who complained that their wives spent too much time in the bath.

Father told me that two of our stable boys had enlisted in the Wehrmacht of their own volition. He said that he missed our cook, even though by the end she was continually singing Yiddish dirges as she baked her challah. We laughed a little.

"Might you have oranges, possibly?" Father asked Fat Franz.

"Certainly we have oranges."

"Could you please make me a screwdriver with fresh-squeezed orange juice?"

"Coming right up," said Franz.

Five minutes later, Franz returned with a downcast look and announced that not one orange could be found in the entire building. "Pardon me, it's the war. They simply disappear."

I saw Stella the moment she stepped out of the elevator. She was wearing the dark dress, and for the first time since she'd been back from Burgstrasse, she appeared in public without her head scarf. Her hair had grown back, and she'd combed a side part into it and set it with water and Brilliantine. Father rose from his stool. As she curtsied, he went a step forward and took her in his arms.

"You splendid girl."

I saw her amazed expression.

"Like a Yazidi princess," he said.

"Very pleased to meet you." I could hear how hard she was trying not to speak in her Berlin dialect.

"And that dress," said Father, pinching the cloth at her waist between his thumb and forefinger. "Florentine silk?"

Stella laughed so loud that two men in the lobby turned to look at her. "Fritz stole it."

Father smiled uncertainly. My ears grew hot.

She linked arms with the two of us and we went into the restaurant.

"Do you like oysters?" asked Father.

"Sorry, what?" asked Stella.

Father ordered a dozen oysters from Sylt on ice; he showed Stella the part of the shell where she should insert the knife. He drizzled vinaigrette over the first one. Oysters, for some reason that wasn't clear to me, were not rationed.

"This looks fun," Stella whispered, and grinned. She slurped the oyster, grimaced at first, then looked in astonishment at my father. "It's really delicious," she said.

"The best ones are from Saint-Malo, straight out of the sea. And with lemon juice," he said.

Maybe it was wonderful only because we knew it would never be like this again. Father spoke of his trips across the Atlantic on the *Queen Mary*. He talked about Melek Taus, whom the Yazidis worshipped, a fallen angel who had extinguished hell's fire with his tears.

Stella sat by Father, eating up his stories. He described a Chinese painting from the fifteenth century that he'd seen in the Metropolitan Museum of Art. It showed a group of apes climbing a tree above a lake and grabbing at the reflection of the world in the water.

"Why?" asked Stella.

"Why do we do what we do, my love?"

A waiter stepped up to the table. Father looked for a long time at the menu the waiter gave him.

"Waiter, what precisely is 'spice meat'?"

"Formerly it was called 'ragout,' sir."

"And 'fire pot'?"

"The French call it 'pot-au-feu,' sir."

"Ah, I see."

"The names of the dishes have been altered according to the instructions of the Reich Ministry for Public Enlightenment, sir."

For a moment I thought of Tristan.

"Because we have to," said Stella.

"Excuse me?" said Father.

"The apes and the world. We do what we do because we have to."

That night Stella smiled a lot, and every now and then she touched Father's arm. As it grew late, they both were chatting about the secret wisdom of the Druse, as I only half listened. She smiled, let her eyes travel the room, and then, from one blink to the next, the color drained from her face, even I could see it.

"My child, have you seen a ghost?" asked Father, and laughed.

I turned around and saw that she was staring at a table in the corner, where a woman in a cotton dress was sitting with a uniformed man with long curls.

"There," she said, "him . . . there."

"What is it, my dear?" asked Father.

The man with the curls had noticed us looking at him. He raised a glass of wine in greeting.

"Get me out of here," Stella whispered. Her fingernails dug into my hand.

I put my arm around her waist and left the restaurant with her.

"I'll explain tomorrow," she said.

Father walked close behind us and gave me a little velvet bag in the lobby.

"For you both," he said, "for the two of you." He smiled uncertainly again. I nodded and stepped into the elevator. Father remained standing in front. "Good night, young lady," he said again. Stella was leaning her face on my shoulder and didn't seem to hear him.

When the door closed, Stella spoke two words in my ear: "The gardener."

She went into the bathroom of our suite and stayed there a long time. I looked inside the velvet bag. There were two identical watches, a flat model with manual winding. The dial was pale with subtle numbers; the logo appeared in the middle: "Precision."

On a slip of paper, Father had written: "I bought these for your mother and me. Perhaps they will bring the two of you better luck. Aristotle said that time and change are inextricably tied to each other. If you don't like them, give them to someone else. Papa."

I thought the watch was a little big for Stella. When I turned it around, I saw that two interlinked rings were engraved on the back.

When Stella came out of the bathroom, her pupils were dilated from Pervitin. She sat next to me on the bed. She was shaking. I held her arm. She looked at the watches in my hand and reached for them.

"From Father," I said.

"For me?" she asked. She put on one of the watches and rubbed the bezel with the fingers of her right hand. "It's so beautiful."

Stella and I took the watches off when we went to bed. Despite the Pervitin, she fell asleep while I was holding her hand. I thought about the man with the curls. I thought about Cioma Schönhaus and Stella's parents. This had to stop.

Before Father left the next day, I went to his room and we looked out the window together. He held my hand. I told him that I had seen the furniture trucks.

"Why did you really come to this place?" asked Father.

We stood beside each other and kept silent.

"Why did you stay with Mother so long?" I asked.

"Because I had made up my mind."

"But you didn't love each other."

"I still love her now."

"But her weaknesses."

"Every single one."

*

Cases #30 and #31:   The K. couple
                      Witness: Elisabeth P.

Witness Elisabeth P. was the concierge of the house at 32 Landsberger Avenue. On the second floor of this house lived a Jewish family named K. The witness said that one morning, a vehicle stopped in front of the door, and the accused and two men in civil dress came out of it. Shortly thereafter the K. couple was taken away in the vehicle. Their subsequent fate is unknown.

P. I / 256

September 1942

Wolfgang Schäuble is born. The commander of Army Group A, Field Marshal Wilhelm List, is fired; Adolf Hitler takes over the direction of the group. In Berlin's Olympic stadium, the German national soccer team loses 2–3 against Sweden. The ninth commandment of Dr. Joseph Goebbels's Ten Commandments for Every National Socialist is issued: "Lead your life in such a way that in a New Germany you will not need to be ashamed." The SS transports thousands of people from the Litzmannstadt ghetto to the death camp of Chelmno; many children are on the trains. At the European Jewish Conference in Vienna, the Viennese NSDAP gauleiter Baldur von Schirach: "Europe is a sacred symbol of humanity. It is the world of heroes, whether they are called Alexander, Caesar, Frederick the Great, or Napoleon; the world of poets from Homer and Dante to Goethe; the world of philosophers from Plato to Kant and Nietzsche; the musical world from Bach to Beethoven, Mozart. How it fills us with pride to acknowledge these names! What can Herr Roosevelt counter it with?" The U.S. President Franklin D. Roosevelt says on September 7 in a fireside chat, "This is the toughest war of all time. We need not leave it to historians of the future to answer the question whether we are tough enough to meet this unprecedented challenge. We can give that answer now. The answer is 'Yes.'"

*

We paid black-market rates and ate oysters and bee sting torte; we drank cognac, drew with charcoal, and listened to swing records, though we rarely danced. Sometimes we managed to forget about Stella's parents. We felt guilty, each in our own way.

I watched mechanics in uniform waiting on the roof of the IG Farben building across from my hotel room. An 88 mm antiaircraft cannon arrived.

The air-raid siren sounded as Stella and I were sitting in the Deutsche Oper, watching *Madama Butterfly*.

Inside the evening's program was a piece of paper that said what to do in case of an air raid, as the theater did not have a shelter. We went to the cellar of a neighboring building.

For an hour we sat in the cellar in evening dress, knee to knee, waiting for the sound of crashing bombs, and Stella whispered in my ear: "No nighttime stroll this time." In the shelter it smelled of cologne.

After we left the cellar, the opera continued, and a mezzosoprano gave three encores and got a standing ovation. Someone began to sing "The Horst-Wessel Song," and at the end the public sang with the singers onstage. Stella clapped to the beat.

On the way home she pulled me to the Spree riverbank, looked out onto the water, and said, "My parents are off the list."

"What?"

"They're still in the Grosse Hamburger Strasse camp, but they won't be on the next train."

"How?"

"I don't know, dear Fritz."

Tears rolled down her face. I held her hand as we stood by the Spree and felt how damp her palm was.

"Are we in this together?" she asked.

Together. There was enough meaning in that word for a lifetime.

"Let's go to Choulex. Home," I said.

"To the house on the lake?"

Stella pressed her wet cheek against mine.

"I think I want to perform again."

I don't know how she could think of singing at a moment like this.

I looked at my wrist. The watch my father had given me shone in the lamplight. I had forgotten to wind it; the hands had stopped.

One night in bed Stella said, "Fritz?"

"Yes?"

"Can we go out with Tristan again?"

At once I was fully awake. "With Tristan?"

"He's our friend."

Stella rolled onto her back and looked at the ceiling. I bent over her and shook my head. "He called you Jew vermin."

"He did not."

"I was there."

"He said Israelite vermin."

A fly was buzzing around the room and kept flying into the windowpanes.

"Can't you at least try to get in touch with him?" asked Stella.

I stood up, went into the bathroom, and started lathering up shaving soap into a foamy mass in a horn bowl. The soap smelled of sunflowers. It was nighttime, I had shaved in the morning, but nothing made sense anymore anyway.

Stella came into the bathroom, brought a stool up to the mirror for me, and pushed down gently on both my shoulders so I would sit. She stood behind me, put one hand on my throat and, with the other, pulled my head back until it rested against her breasts. She lathered my face with the warm foam in circular motions. Then she picked up the razor.

"Are you afraid again?" she asked. She attempted a laugh.

I saw how her hand trembled. Slowly she drew the blade across my skin.

"Me, too," said Stella. I tried to hold still when she nicked me.

When she was done, blood flowed from several small cuts on my skin. I slid the alum stone all over until they closed up.

"So, Tristan."

She hugged me from behind.

We met a couple of days later in a bar on Lehrter Street in Moabit. Tristan wore a double-breasted suit with pinstripes and, over that, a raincoat.

Tristan was drinking beer from a small glass. He kissed Stella Swiss style—three times on the cheeks—looked at me over her shoulder, and raised his eyebrows high, as if he were trying to tell me something. Then he hugged me and said, "How I've missed you, old boy. How are you feeling?"

Tristan talked for a long time, about how he'd recently been drinking a special herbal concoction called "Herve" a lot, about how he'd been learning how to cook, and about the clay owls he'd added to his collection. He'd also found a new intermediary who smuggled Camembert to Berlin for him in a double-bottomed briefcase.

"Your hair looks excellent now," he said to Stella, and patted the back of her head. His fingers touched her neck, where her hair was soft.

I drank my beer quickly, went to the men's room, took the hand towel from the hook, soaked it in cold water, and laid it on my neck.

When I came back into the taproom, Stella and Tristan were standing so close together that their upper arms touched. I saw them through the cigarette smoke and stood still at the doorframe. They looked serious; Stella kept shaking her head. Then she caught sight of me and smiled.

"What's going on?" I asked.

"Ah, old boy," said Tristan, "I just said that I would like so much to go to the front. Did you know that I'm a fighter pilot? Battle wing."

A cold drop of water rolled from my shirt down my spine.

We went on foot to the Melodie Klub. Stella hooked her arms through ours, like she'd done on our first night out. The asphalt glistened with rain.

I had drunk quickly because I thought it would make things simpler, which is never true. The freckled barmaid greeted Tristan with a kiss on the mouth. There were lots of patrons in the club. Most of the men were wearing double-breasted pin-striped suits like Tristan. The cigar smoke made my eyes tear up.

Stella danced with her cheek next to mine. She drank cognac and kirsch mixed together. When the freckled barmaid set out a metal box of cocaine on the bar, we took some of it from a spoon. I became alert, though my nose was numb, but the feeling persisted that my life was out of balance. Tristan shoveled up a heaping spoonful for Stella out of the box and held her chin in his other hand as she inhaled.

"Why don't you sing, little Kristin?" asked Tristan. My stomach cramped when he called her that.

"Gladly."

"Shall we sing a duet? Yes?"

Stella looked at me.

"Old boy, may I carry off your girl for a short while?"

I thumped Tristan too hard on the shoulder.

He and Stella went onto the dance floor, danced a quick Charleston, then Tristan gave the band a signal, made a standing jump onto the stage, and stretched his hand out to Stella. As she climbed up, a beam of light from a ceiling lamp landed on the dial of her watch.

Tristan and Stella sang a song in English. He sang slightly out of tune, but it didn't seem to bother him. She kept looking at me and smiling at me over the heads of the dancers.

*

Cases #23 to #27:   *Gerda K.*
                              Elly L.
                              Aron P. with 2 sons
                              Witnesses: 1. Gerda K., 2. Elly L.

The witness Gerda K. had come to visit Aron P. when she saw the accused standing in the courtyard, looking at the P. apartment. The witness hastily retreated from the scene and reported her observation to witness Elly L. That evening she visited Aron P. and communicated this to him. P., however, tried to allay her concerns. On the following day, when the two witnesses called again for P., the door was opened by the Jewish investigators B. and L., with the words, "Good evening, Frau K., you are under arrest." Both witnesses were taken to the Grosse Hamburger Strasse camp. During the interrogation, SS chief Dobberke asked the witness K. to identify three more illegal Jewish residents, in order to be sent to Theresienstadt instead of Auschwitz. The witness refused this request. The accused was present at one interrogation with Dobberke. As she prepared to leave the room, Dobberke asked, "And where might you be going today?" She said, "To the theater." Dobberke retorted cynically, "Break a leg!" The accused was wearing, as in numerous other cases, a green suit and a hunting cap. P. and his sons went to Auschwitz. The sons live today in Australia, but the whereabouts of the father are unknown.

Pp. 1/107, 193–194
Pp. 1/17, 42, 192

October 1942

In B1a, the women's camp in Birkenau, SS members carry out a selection; subsequently two thousand female prisoners will die in the gas chamber. The German people are ordered to gather beechnuts for the extraction of cooking oil. From a speech by Hermann Göring in Berlin's Sport Palace: "If the war is lost, you are destroyed. The Jew stands with his inexhaustible hatred behind these thoughts of destruction." The death sentence against seventeen-year-old Helmuth Hübener is carried out; his offense was distributing leaflets containing information from British news reports. On the grounds of the army testing facility at Peenemünde, on the Baltic island of Usedom, the successful launch of the V-2, the first long-range guided ballistic missile in the world. In Italy the manufacture of toys is forbidden; toy factories henceforth must produce war material. Tana Berghausen is born in the Schlosshof camp in Bielefeld. Her mother gets onto a train soon after and rides with her for forty hours in a cattle car to Auschwitz; on the platform SS soldiers beat the infant Tana Berghausen to death. The dates of death of her parents, who were also killed at Auschwitz, are unknown. The tenth commandment of Dr. Joseph Goebbels's Ten Commandments for Every National Socialist is issued: "Believe in the future; that is the only way you will win it."

*

In the mornings we lay beside each other and waited until it was light.

"When will we go to Choulex, Tink?"

"Don't know."

"But I've got a Swiss passport. Let's just go."

The pause was too long. I liked the way Stella smelled when she was sleeping.

"You think you deserve something better," she said.

"What?"

"I have to save my parents."

"But how?"

"Tristan says he'll help me."

I kept silent.

"He's doing the same thing with the singing," she said.

"With the singing?"

"You don't get it."

"Stella, nobody is singing here anymore."

"I am permitted to sing at Christmas at Wannsee, in the big mansion where we went last spring."

"At Schwanenwerder?"

"But just one song this time."

"Under the swastika flag?"

"Am I supposed to be ashamed now?"

I said nothing more. Her breathing was loud.

"I'm sorry, Fritz."

"For what?"

"For everything."

I stroked the skin under her breasts. "Please don't sing."

"One song."

"Please, Stella."

She reached behind her back between my legs, but I didn't react.

Stella fell asleep. I tried to do the same.

On my last visit to Tristan's apartment, before I had even taken off my coat, I raised the question I should have asked him long before. He smiled enigmatically and beautifully. He had decorated the whole apartment with vases full of white gladioli.

"What are you doing, Tristan?"

"Hmm," he said. He stretched his long arms until he could almost touch both walls of his hallway with his fingertips. He turned around, went to the kitchen, and sat on a stool by the table. In front of him was a bowl of broad beans. Tristan reached in and separated the good from the bad, looked up at me and said, "Madagascar."

"Madagascar?"

"It has a special ring to it, doesn't it?"

Tristan's hands scrabbled through the beans as he told me in an energetic, enthusiastic voice that he was working on something called the "Madagascar Plan." All the Jews from the German Reich would be taken down to the coast of Africa and, from there, move to the savannas of Madagascar. "Relocation," Tristan called it.

"There are thousands of plants and animals and everything, and nobody will bother them," he said.

"In Madagascar?"

"They've got lemurs there, for example. Excellent creatures."

"You're working on shipping the Jews to Africa?"

He nodded, stuck a raw broad bean in his mouth, stood up, and slapped both his hands on my shoulders. "Madagascar, that's the task they've set me, old boy."

"What about Stella?"

"What does it have to do with her?"

"Will she also go to Madagascar?"

"We're turning her into an honorary Aryan, didn't she tell you?"

Tristan got the épées from the neighboring room and tossed the protective clothing at my feet.

"It's great that you're here," he said.

I laid the fencing jacket on a kitchen chair. I lifted the épée. It was dull at the tip, but not too dull.

"You know, I've thought a lot about what the difference is between you and me," said Tristan. He put on his fencing mask. "I mean, why you can't manage to get away from Stella."

Tristan left his fencing jacket open. He walked a couple of meters backward from the kitchen into the dining room; I followed him. Tristan did footwork exercises as he spoke.

171

"It probably comes down to your nature, not that you'd particularly like to hear that."

He feinted a couple times.

"I mean, if you have thin blood, you're weak, right?" He pushed up his fencing mask, his fair hair stuck to his forehead. "Forgive me, old boy, if I'm being too frank now. But if I ever had a girlfriend and someone did to her what they did to Kristin—I mean, if someone hurt her that badly, with the hair and everything—believe me, that man would not live long."

He raised his épée in the air.

"And if my girlfriend had an entire country against her, then I would ride with a torch through that country and burn it to the ground, house by house. I mean, one way or another, family is the most important thing. It's really great the way little Kristin protects her family. You should be happy about that."

The fragrance of the flowers filled the room. Dust motes hovered in the light of the autumn sun. I had not known before then what it felt like to hate.

"Why did you speak to me at the Melodie Klub, that first time?" I asked.

"House by house," said Tristan.

I took the épée and walked to the fencing strip. Tristan stood tall and straight in front of me.

For the first time I heard something like uncertainty in his voice.

"Because I thought you might be different," he said.

I came so near to him that I touched the grille of his mask with my nose. Behind it I saw his eyes. This time I didn't cross my hands behind my back to hide their trembling. My fingers closed on the grip of the épée.

"Is everything all right?" asked Tristan.

"Fine," I said, and looked through the grille. For a couple of breaths we stood there like that.

"Somehow it sounds like you don't really mean that," said Tristan.

I kept silent.

"Be honest with me, Fritz."

I turned around and left. I rammed the épée into the glass frame where the black feather hung. The glass splintered. The épée didn't stick; it fell to the floor. What happened to the feather, I don't know. Tristan called after me, but he didn't try to stop me.

"Come on, Friedrich, stay. I had Camembert brought in specially."

November 1942

The Red Army surrounds the German 6th Army at Stalingrad. 492 people burn to death in a fire at the Boston nightclub Cocoanut Grove when a broken lightbulb emits sparks and sets the decor on fire. The Polish underground fighter and courier Jan Kozielewski, alias Jan Karski, brings reports of the deportations from Warsaw and the death camps to the Polish government-in-exile in London. The German national soccer team defeats Slovakia 5–2; it will be the last game of the German national soccer team until 1950. A cease-fire ends the battle between the Allies and Vichy troops in North Africa. After a British air raid on Berlin, the Deutsche Bank building burns down, among many others. In contradiction of Hitler's orders to hold the German position in North Africa at any price, Field Marshal Erwin Rommel withdraws his troops after the defeat at El Alamein. At the Vigorelli Velodrome in Milan, the Italian bicyclist Fausto Coppi breaks the hour world record, 45.871 kilometers, by 31 meters. In Leipzig an office opens for "those disfigured and disabled by war, those blinded by war, and other blind people." Heinrich Himmler orders the Reich University in Strasbourg to create a collection of Jewish skulls and skeletons. To this end, some one hundred Jews travel from Auschwitz to Strasbourg.

*

I found Stella's revolver among my shirts in the wardrobe. I went to the nightstand and took from the drawer the bullet Tristan had given me. I hid the loaded weapon in the back of my pants, walked to 28 Burgstrasse, and waited across from the entrance to the Jewish Affairs office until the gardener finished his workday. It was an unremarkable building on the bank of the Spree, directly around the corner from the old Busch circus. In front of the entry tower stood a watchman in an SS uniform with a rifle over his shoulder.

The gardener came through the main door at 4:32, stopped to talk with a colleague, and laughed so loud that I could hear him on the other side of the street.

In Münzstrasse the gardener carried a baby carriage up the steps of a house entrance for a woman. He parted from his colleague with an embrace and entered a tavern. I followed him. He drank tea at the bar and chatted with the innkeeper. In a corner I ate watery bean stew so as not to attract attention.

When the innkeeper disappeared into the kitchen, I got up and sat on the empty stool next to the gardener. The cocked revolver was in my jacket pocket.

The gardener looked at me over the rims of his glasses. "Good afternoon," he said.

"Look at my right hand," I said too quickly. "I have a gun."

The gardener smiled. "What do you want from me?" He spoke Bavarian German.

"Why did you torture Stella?"

"Torture?"

"Why?"

The man acted like he was talking to a friend. "We just talked about dahlias."

"What?"

"Dahlias, such majestic flowers."

I was speechless for a moment.

"You certainly have to distinguish between varieties."

The innkeeper came out of the kitchen and looked at us. I took the revolver out of my pocket and pushed it against the gardener's throat from below. The innkeeper jumped back into the kitchen and knocked over a jar of pickled eggs in the process, which shattered on the floor behind the bar.

"Why did you hurt her?"

"It's too bad about the pickled eggs. Hurt who?" asked the gardener.

"Stella Goldschlag."

"Oh," he said, and smiled. "The blond poison."

"What's that supposed to mean?"

"That's what the Jews of Berlin call her. Didn't you know?"

He looked at me. I held his gaze.

"How could you do what you did?"

"What?"

"Beat someone with a rubber hose?"

"Oh, that." He paused. "Well." Carefully he reached for his teacup. "May I?" he asked.

He was drinking chamomile tea. The revolver was pressed against his throat, but he swallowed.

"The Jews have waged war on the whole world for centuries. It's only logical that now we are fighting back."

"How do you sleep at night?"

He laughed and smacked his lips twice. "You fool, do you know why they call me the gardener?"

His laughter was unbearable.

"Do you know anyone who enjoys weeding?"

"What?"

"Everyone likes to sit in the garden and look at the lilacs. The daisies and the begonias. But think of the weeds—nobody planted them, nobody cares about them. Plenty of idiots think that all that's wrong with weeds is that they're not pretty to look at. I say it's more than that: they don't belong here, they're a blight to our nature and a threat to our native gardens and forests."

"Shut up."

"Look here, think of invasive species. Nature doesn't want them to grow here. I think nature must preserve its order. Yet here they are. So, now what? Should I put on gloves to carefully pluck them out of the German soil, roots and all, and put them on a ship back where they came from? You do that and they won't survive anyway. So, I pick up the spade at once. It's best for everyone: for the plants that don't belong here and for nature, because then she's all pure again. It's totally logical."

He continued smiling.

"Do you love your Fatherland?"

177

"My fatherland? I'm Swiss."

"Do you love your fatherland?"

"No."

"I will pray for you tonight," he said. "And now stand up. Put away your toy. Walk backward to the door and then get out of here, and I don't ever want to see you again."

He said it calmly.

"As for Goldschlag, nobody forces her to do anything. She is, in her twisted way, truer to her Fatherland than either of us." The gardener raised his fingers carefully, plucked a fallen eyelash from my cheek, and said, "You can make a wish."

He nodded to me.

"Be happy that I'm in a good mood today. Now beat it."

Maybe another man would have shot the gardener in the throat that day. Another man would have punched him in the face and broken his jaw or taken a shard of the pickled egg jar and slashed his jugular. Maybe Tristan would have done it.

I had come to this country because I had wanted the strength of the Germans to pass to me. I had admired the Germans. I had admired Tristan.

Slowly I stood up and walked backward to the door.

I was not a German, I was not Tristan; and if that was strength, I knew now that I did not want to be strong.

Perhaps it's our own weaknesses that lead us to hurt others.

I was a young man from Switzerland who missed his father, who loved a Jewish woman, and whose most courageous act had been to carry an old billy goat down a mountain. I didn't understand what was happening in Germany, why bombs were falling, why Jews had to be hated, and why I had been drawn into this war.

But I knew on this day that I had never been invisible.

"Wait a second, you dope," said the gardener.

I paused. He raised his index finger.

"Your aftershave. What is it? I like it."

I ran. I stuck the revolver in my pocket and ran as fast as I could. The gardener remained seated, drinking his tea.

She kissed me on the neck in greeting. The back of my shirt was wet with sweat. I took a shower; she dabbed the water off my skin. As I lay beside her in bed I asked, "How did you get your parents off the list for good?"

"What do you mean?"

"How, Stella?"

She understood; I saw it in her face. Her features relaxed. "I did what was right."

"I know."

"You know nothing."

She got up, took a Juno from her cigarette case, and stood in front of the closed window as she smoked.

"Your watch isn't ticking anymore," she said.

"Stella, I need to know the truth."

"Why isn't it ticking?"

I took the lamp with the porcelain base from the night table and threw it across the room at the silk wallpaper.

Stella looked at me. She walked around the bed, picked up the broken pieces and threw them in the wastebasket. She sat beside me on the mattress. She held a shard in her hand.

"I will tell you everything"—she drew a breath—"and then you will leave me."

I looked at her mouth and waited. I was no longer afraid.

"And then you'll leave me," she repeated, and nodded.

As she spoke, it was as if she were looking through me. She told me everything.

I stood up. Her voice was barely audible.

"Tell your children about me sometime. Will you do that?"

Stella's hands were on her lap, closed around the shard; her shoulders had fallen forward, her strength had drained away.

I sank to my knees before her and looked up from below into her eyes. Stella let her head fall forward and touch me.

Her forehead against mine.

I realized I didn't have to say anything. We were together.

This woman contained so many roles within herself: the artist's model, the singer with the breathy voice, the beauty in my bathtub, the penitent, the liar, the victim. Stella Gold-schlag, the woman I loved.

I don't know if it's wrong to betray one human being to save another.

I don't know if it's right to betray one human being to save another.

I wanted to crawl away somewhere. I knew I wasn't prepared to reckon with this fate. But even stronger than that, to my surprise, was a feeling of closeness to Stella, of solidarity with her. She did things that made other people hate her, and I stayed by her. I didn't understand her, and yet, I stayed.

With everyone else she played a role. But with me she was at home. When we were together, we were the only people in the world. At one point she said, "Even worse than fear is loneliness."

Her hands lay on my neck.

"This cannot continue," I said.

I could feel it on my forehead when she lightly shook her head.

December 1942

Heinrich Himmler orders the deportation of all Roma and Sinti living in Germany to Auschwitz-Birkenau. The German press reminds readers of the sensible parameters of blackout periods: "When it's time, turn out the light! Spare power by day to make nights bright!" In the *Börsenblatt*, the financial publication of the German book trade, booksellers are encouraged to empty their storerooms to increase the supply of books at Christmas. The wage tax cards for the year 1942 will remain valid in 1943 to save paper. The writer and theologian Jochen Klepper, his Jewish wife, and his stepdaughter commit suicide to save themselves from the concentration camp. Richard Wagner's opera *Lohengrin* is performed at the opening of the Japanese harvest festival. The Reich Ministry of Public Enlightenment and Propaganda issues a decree commandeering private theaters in Berlin. Because of the growing shortage of raw materials, the German press exhorts housewives: "Spare soap—go easy on the washing!" and to that end, to wash clothes only every five weeks. Alice Schwarzer is born. The Royal Air Force begins systematically bombing Berlin. In Chicago, the physicist Enrico Fermi conducts the first human-made sustained nuclear chain reaction.

*

We spent the nights in the bunker and slept sitting up. In the cellar, no fiddlers played anymore.

We heard the flak fire of the 88 mm antiaircraft guns through the ceiling. When an incendiary bomb fell on the building next door, the pressure waves sent chalk flying off the bunker walls, producing a cloud that blinded us for a few minutes. I coughed up phlegm all day long.

Stella often went out on her own in the city. She wore a leather coat on her outings. We didn't talk about what she was doing.

A few nights still belonged just to us. When no bombs were falling, she lay against me, tucked into my hollow, as she had called it once, and stroked my arm. I didn't want to fall asleep, because then I wouldn't be able to smell her anymore.

In the morning she sang. For her performance at Wannsee she prepared three songs.

"Tristan says if it goes well, I'll get a regular night at Café Nanu. He's getting me an Aryan certificate for the Reich Music Chamber."

"So he says."

"They'll stamp my name on the outside."

"Isn't that dangerous?"

"Why would it be dangerous?"

"Because you're Jewish."

Stella gave a little laugh. She said, "Have you ever asked yourself whether there might be a reason that everybody hates the Jews?"

"What does 'Neschume' mean?" I asked.

She came up to me. I thought she was going to hit me. The word stirred something inside her that she hid behind smiles in her everyday life.

"Where did you hear that?" Her Berlin dialect had vanished. She spoke in accent-free High German.

"From you," I said.

"I never said that."

"In your sleep."

"You're lying."

Stella came up close to me. I looked into her wide pupils.

"I can't get a sense of you anymore," she said. "I no longer feel sure of you."

"You're speaking High German."

She smiled wearily. I didn't know what would be left of this woman if I stripped away all the lies.

"Could you speak it all along?"

"Oh, Fritz."

She took a deep breath.

I finally understood. There comes a time in every love when it is too late for answers.

"Neschume," I said.

"Stop it, you really don't know what you're saying."

"Neschume."

Her lips glistened. "Fritz, what have we done?"

I could taste the salt of the tears that rolled down her upper lip. I lifted Stella up and set her on the secretary desk by the easel.

If I could draw her, I would draw her that way. The way she sat on the desk, her hands clasped behind my neck, her back dropped low, and her head tilted back against the window glass.

"Please don't sing," I said.

"Neschume," she said, and when she said it, it sounded right.

"Stella, are you listening to me?"

"It's Yiddish."

She was warm again, and soft. I kept quiet.

"It means 'soul.'"

It rained in Berlin on Christmas Eve that year. There was a Christmas tree in the lobby of the Grand Hotel with lit candles on it. Stella was still asleep when I left the hotel in the morning and took a walk through the city. In the Tiergarten I saw women gathering firewood.

Back in the hotel I went to the bar and ordered breakfast from Franz. By now, many kinds of food were scarce in the hotel, but if you had enough money, the waiters could still find real coffee to bring you.

I went into our room and stroked Stella's foot, which was sticking out from under the covers. She was still lying down when two men in livery brought out the table and set it.

"What should I bring you?" I asked.

"Fritz?"

"Yes."

"You are so sweet."

"Coffee?"

"Yes, and a roll with jam."

I put two spoonfuls of jam on each half, the way she liked it.

"Today's the day," she said, as she sat up and set her cup on the covers.

We lay in bed and listened to the rain pattering on the copper window ledge. As I felt the pressure of Stella's hands, I thought that in the end maybe everything might turn out all right.

In the afternoon we took a bath together with lots of soap. Then she sat naked in front of the mirror and put on her makeup. I took the buffalo horn comb, which once had belonged to my mother, and combed Stella's hair.

I stammered, "The truth, it isn't like hibiscus."

"What?"

"Hibiscus."

Stella put away her rouge sponge, threw both her arms around my legs, and pulled herself up to me.

"All right," she said. All right. The rouge left a mark on my pants.

When Stella was in the bath again, I went to the wardrobe and brought the revolver out from its hiding place among the shirts.

The taxi ride took a long time. Stella sat beside me; she slid back and forth on the seat cushions, singing scales. The driver, drinking beer from a bottle, kept looking into the rearview mirror and said, "I don't know you, but pipe down."

Stella fell silent. For a moment we heard only the rain on the roof of the car.

"My lady friend is a singer," I said. "She has a performance shortly, so please shut your mouth."

Stella grabbed my forefinger and squeezed it.

"It's all my fault," she said softly. I felt her breath on my neck.

"There's no question of blame here," I said.

We arrived late. Tristan rushed up to us in the driveway. A flag heavy with rain hung from a pole. Tristan greeted Stella with kisses.

"Merry Christmas and Heil Hitler."

He shook my hand and gave my shoulder a squeeze.

"Come by again sometime," he said.

Stella looked beautiful that night, I want to say that once again. The year had taken away her softness. She had grown too thin. She wore hardly any makeup, and she'd had a wave put in her fair hair; soon it would be long enough for a bun again. On her wrist she wore the watch Father had given her. In heels, Stella was taller than me.

The villa smelled of gingerbread, beeswax, and pine needles. Tristan led Stella through the rooms. All the guests looked at her. She wasn't playing a role, I understood, as I leaned against the wallpaper, watching her and Tristan as they walked through the room. When she would go out into the city in her leather jacket, I would tell myself, That's not who she really is. But now I understood that it wasn't that simple. That was part of who she was. And so was this.

Waiters served Russian vodka, which the guests took as a great joke. Stella didn't drink.

When she leaned against the wallpaper near me, she whispered in my ear, "Please don't say anything now."

I nodded. She kissed my cheek. She was wearing her watch on her left wrist; I wore mine on my right. It made a clicking noise when the watch faces knocked against each other.

I did not want to look at Stella anymore. She reached for my chin and turned my face to hers.

"Do you hate me now?" she asked.

She laid her hands on my cheeks and ran her thumb across my scar. The light from the chandeliers was reflected in her pupils.

"So, I guess I'm up."

"Good luck," I said.

She nodded. "Thank you for this year."

Stella walked through the crowd to a small stage that had been built in front of the glass facade to the garden. A piano stood there, and a microphone on a metal stand. The lake lay behind it in the night.

Stella stepped onto the stage, the pianist nodded to her. The guests fell silent; many were in uniform, some of the men wore knickerbockers. Almost all of them had swastika armbands tied to their right arms. I felt the revolver in the waistband of my trousers.

The pianist played a jazzy version of "The Night Is Not Only for Sleeping." At the other end of the room I saw Tristan on the stairway, tapping with his feet. Stella gripped the microphone stand in both hands.

It was a good song for her, with her breathy Berlin accent. She sang the song as I would never hear it sung again.

As the pianist played the last note, the audience fell silent for a couple of seconds before applause broke out. At that moment, Stella was where she wanted to be.

In Grosse Hamburger Strasse, Toni and Gerhard Goldschlag crouched on the floor and maybe held hands.

I will never leave you, I promise.

"Betrayal" is a big word.

For the next song, Stella sang the Deutschlandlied, and after a couple of notes all the men sang along.

She paused a moment before the third song, as if she were mulling something over, but I knew she had made her decision long before. She looked across the room and nodded to me. She said, "Thank you for letting me live." A few guests glanced at one another; a couple murmured to each other; a few laughed as if she had made a joke. A woman raised her right arm. The pianist played the first chords of "Stardust." For the rest of my life I would hear that song. I listened as Stella sang:

> Sometimes I wonder
> Why I spend the lonely nights
> Dreaming of a song
> The melody
> Haunts my reverie
> And I am once again with you
> When our love was new
> And each kiss an inspiration
> But that was long ago
> Now my consolation is in the stardust of a song.

She looked at me as I pushed off from the wallpaper and walked back through the rows of seats to the door. I could not see any change in her face, but I knew that she saw me. Her notes sounded clear.

Drivers stood outside smoking.

"Where to?"

I heard applause before I pulled the door of the car shut.

"Anhalter Station, please."

I knew that every Thursday, a night train traveled south, and I hoped that also held true on Christmas Eve. It probably did; the Germans liked their schedules. I didn't drive back to the Grand Hotel. I took nothing with me. I had come to this city because I thought it was important that I separate the rumors from the truth, and now I was fleeing it. I left no letter behind and told nobody I would see them again, because there would be no again.

As we crossed the Spree, I told the chauffeur to stop. I got out, took the revolver from my waistband and dropped it into the water.

The train was at the platform. I bought a ticket for a private cabin from the conductor. Then I walked to one of the pushcart salesmen outside the station and bought a bag of apples. I left my remaining food ration tickets with the vendor.

As the train rolled away, I thought of the life I would not live.

I would be able to distract myself, marry someone else, and act as if Stella had never existed. I would laugh. I would get drunk and talk about her as if she had been my trophy, even though I knew that the opposite was true. I would be able to say at the end of my life that I measured my happiness not by how much I had been loved, but by how much I had loved. I would try to forget her. Life turns us into liars.

Every bottle of champagne reminds me of her, every apple, every piece of coal, every nude, every jazz standard, every chocolate, every night of dancing, the word "Berlin," the word "hotel," the word "Jew."

I thought about the woman who wore a Tyrolean hunting cap, perched at an angle, sometimes a dark silk dress from Chanel and sometimes a leather coat. A girl, twenty-one years old, who answered to the name Kristin and was named Stella Ingrid Goldschlag.

I thought about a liar. I didn't know how many people she had betrayed—a hundred, two hundred. I thought of you.

You, with the gap in your teeth and your soft, thick hair. We would have married in April at the lake. I would have built you a theater and stolen sequined dresses for you. You would have danced Viennese waltzes with me, unconfident but happy. You would have been the mother of my children. We would have held hands in the park. I would have taken the Orient Express with you to Istanbul and drunk sugary coffee in the bazaar with you. You would have painted the walls of our house in many colors. We would have sung silly songs on car rides together. Every morning you would have woken in my arms, and I would never have let you go. I would have told you the truth.

The train rolled on. I untied my bow tie and put it in the inside pocket of my dinner jacket. My fingertips touched a note.

Father was wrong. Sometimes there is such a thing as blame.

I looked out the window at the lights of Berlin and knew that for me something would always be missing. But I was also grateful. You would remain my first happy memory. Thank you for showing me what love is.

The bag of apples lay in my lap as the train sped up and headed south.

Little by little the lights of the city faded, until we were going too fast and there was no going back, and Germany lay in darkness.

I opened the window a crack, took the note from the inside pocket of my dinner jacket and threw it into the wind.

*

Question: What blame do you assign yourself, considering your confessions on file?

Answer: When I read in the newspapers that I had brought misfortune to so many women, men, and children, it troubled me very greatly, then I consulted my conscience and came to the conviction that my only guilt, and the only crime I committed, was letting myself, as a Jewish woman, take part in field work for the Gestapo. I note, however, that I undertook this work not of my own volition. As far as I recall, I voluntarily described all the cases I know of. But it is too long ago for me to remember every detail exactly. For the time being, I have no further information to give.

March 8, 1946
Berlin Criminal Commissariat, Department KJ F-zbV-

A Note from the Author

Friedrich is a fictional character. Tristan von Appen is a fictional character. The Nazi government's Madagascar Plan was real and was permanently shelved in 1939.

Walter Dobberke worked until the end of the war in the detention camp on Grosse Hamburger Strasse. In 1945, he died of diphtheria in a Soviet prisoner of war camp in Poznan. The mucus membranes of his pharynx and larynx swelled; his respiratory track narrowed. Dobberke suffocated.

Cioma Schönhaus fled Berlin by bicycle in 1943 into Switzerland. He used his best papers to accomplish this, a forged military ID card, and with it succeeded in passing every checkpoint. In Basel, with the help of a stipend, he completed his education in graphic design and later worked in that field. He had four sons and lived to be ninety-two years old.

Toni and Gerhard Goldschlag were forced in 1943 to board a train to Auschwitz, where they were killed.

Joseph Goebbels declared Berlin free of Jews on June 19, 1943.

Stella Goldschlag worked for the Gestapo even after the death of her parents. She never explained why she continued to hunt Jews after her parents were gassed.

She married five times. None of the marriages lasted. Goldschlag gave birth to a daughter in 1945. The identity of the father was never confirmed.

After the war, Goldschlag tried to register in Berlin as a victim of fascism. Berlin Jews recognized her and had her arrested. On May 31, 1946, a Soviet military tribunal sentenced her to ten years in prison as an accessory to murder.

Goldschlag's daughter was adopted by a Jewish family and moved to Israel. She refused to have any contact with her biological mother.

It could never be established how many Jews Goldschlag betrayed to the Gestapo. Most of her victims were dead when the prosecutor brought the indictment. The number is likely many hundreds of people.

In the year 1957, after serving her sentence, Goldschlag received a new indictment, this time from the Criminal Court in Moabit, and was sentenced to ten years in prison. As she already had been punished for her crimes, she was permitted to remain in freedom. The witness statements cited in the novel come from those proceedings. In the year 1994, Stella Goldschlag jumped out of a window in her apartment in Freiburg, hit the concrete, and died.

Acknowledgments

Thank you to the man who decided this book should be read in English, Peter Blackstock, my editor at Grove Atlantic.

Thank you to Liesl Schillinger, who translated this book so beautifully and without whom I would not have a voice in English.

Thank you, N.K., for going over this book with me. You are marvelous.

*

"All Through the Night" (from Anything Goes). Words and music by Cole Porter. Copyright © 1934 (renewed) WC Music Corp. All rights reserved. Used by permission of Alfred Music.

"Stardust." Music by Hoagy Carmichael. Words by Mitchell Parish. Copyright © 1929 (Renewed) EMI Mills Music, Inc., Songs of Peer, Ltd, and Reservoir Media Music. Exclusive worldwide print rights for EMI Mills Music, Inc. administered by Alfred Music. All rights reserved. Used By Permission of Alfred Music for 50% control in the USA and Australia and 100% control in the rest of the world. U.S. print rights administered by Songs of Peer, Ltd. Copyright renewed. Used by permission. All rights reserved. All rights for Reservoir Media Music administered in the British Reversionary Territories by Reservoir Media Management, Inc. All rights reserved. Used by permission. Reprinted by Permission of Hal Leonard LLC.